STONE VALLEY SERIES:

A Place in His Heart

The Wilderness Bride

The Lady of North Star

Sand Castles

The Crossing

STONE VALLEY SERIES:

Book #2

THE WILDERNESS BRIDE

By

DONNA WHITAKER

All scripture quotations are taken from the
King James Version of the Bible.

Dedication:

To all my dear grandchildren.

CHAPTER ONE

Staring out the window of her cabin, gazing appreciatively at the land that was now hers...North Star...and what she had accomplished in such a short time, Rachel's mind wandered back to the day when she and husband Ransom started their journey from Virginia to settle in Stone Valley, Kentucky. Traveling on the Wilderness Road had brought still another abrupt transformation in her ever-changing life. This journey to Green River Country had been her salvation...a new life, a new start. Yet—it had cost her...more than others really knew. Had it been just a few short months ago since they left Virginia? Rachel Templeton was only seventeen-years-old, but it seemed an eon ago.

Wellington, Virginia...1793

IT WAS AUGUST and, although it was normally dry during this time of the season, the morning had been wet and wild with rain.

The oak trees etched themselves against the sky, bending their limbs as the big drops fell, and the wind skulked restlessly in the tops of the trees.

A young woman, married, but not yet out of her teens, sat by the parlor window, the mending in her hands forgotten, as she watched the lightning flash and heard its corresponding thunder.

She was a striking girl, often described by some as beautiful, with long, dark waves cascading down her back and eyes that matched the color of her hair. Eyes…that, at this moment, were as restless as the storm that raged outside.

Her husband was at the sawmill helping his brothers get equipment crated up to ship on the Ohio River. She loved the smell of newly-sawn wood and had spent some of her best hours there as he taught her some of his woodworking skills.

Wishing she were at the mill with him, it was hard to concentrate on her stitching, and she kept staring at the window, as though the pelting rain would magically stop, and she could finagle some excuse to leave the confines of the room.

The other ladies in the room kept up a stream of constant chatter, but, so intent was the attention of the girl on the storm, she barely heard them.

"Rachel, you must watch the stitches you make," said Elizabeth Templeton, as she inspected Rachel's sewing.

Reluctantly, Rachel drew her eyes and thoughts from outside and turned to find Elizabeth bending over the handiwork in her lap.

"Smaller ones," Elizabeth gently advised. "You know…like I taught you," holding up her own sewing as an example.

Rachel's gaze slipped to the garment in her hands and saw how poor her stitching really was. It was her husband's shirt. "But Ransom wouldn't care," she thought and nearly conveyed that thought into spoken words, but bit her tongue in time.

She loved her mother-in-law, but honestly!

With most of their belongings packed in crates and stacked all around them, ready to be shipped down the Ohio River to the Falls in Kentucky, what difference did it make whether this day of the week was kept as their sewing and mending day?

After all, they were leaving soon for Kentucky. What difference did it make to sew a new dress as Elizabeth was doing? Goodness knows, she had plenty of dresses already.

For that matter, why sew at all?

"But, Elizabeth," Rachel complained, frowning at the clumsy mending she grasped in her hands, "with so much to do, why waste time on sewing?"

Even as she spoke, there was a rumble of thunder that captured her attention again.

Elizabeth gave her a look, her eyes faintly amused. Try as she would to teach her—sewing did not come easily to Rachel. Cooking, either, for that matter, for she despised anything domestic.

"Now, Rachel," Elizabeth said, drawing the girl's attention, once again, from the window, "we must maintain order and schedule," she explained patiently. "We've discussed the value of discipline many times."

Rachel, irritated at being house-bound, pressed her lips together to hold back a comment, as Elizabeth once again made known the merits of a regimented life. Elizabeth discussed; she listened…as always.

Elizabeth was right, of course. But Rachel didn't like Elizabeth's idea of a disciplined life.

Her mother hadn't made her sew or cook while she was alive. Her childhood was spent out-of-doors, hunting and fishing, or working the land with her father. Not that the work wasn't hard. It was.

However, there was nothing like an afternoon breeze on a hot day that made you stop whatever you were doing, and turn your face into the wind, or—at the spur of the moment—go for a swim in the river.

Her mother-in-law just didn't understand and neither did the people of this town.

Rachel sighed, nodded, and rubbed her knuckle briefly against her head. Taking the scissors Elizabeth was offering her, she began to snip at her clumsy stitches.

Frustrated, Rachel mentally clicked off the endless socials, the afternoon teas, and numerous church committees she had been expected to participate in. She hated it—all of it! She'd never learned the art of polite conversation and felt awkward, never quite fitting in with these people of so-called refinement.

Above all—the dreaded Wellington Ladies' Sewing Circle, held once a month, was a great source of embarrassment to her. Her sewing was horrible and, already sensing they talked unkindly about her behind her back, one day she overheard Beatrice Bennett and Eliza Hardin whispering about her handiwork for the orphans' bazaar.

Rachel had stitched a lap quilt and was quite proud of her hard work. But upon hearing their remarks that her stitches were "as crooked as the Indian trail tree in Cooper's Grove", she looked a little closer at the quilt in her hands and realized they were right. Crestfallen, and suppressing a sigh, she was afraid that she would never learn!

With a wounded glance at Beatrice and Eliza that caught the malicious grins on their faces, Rachel bristled. They might be right about her sewing, but they had no right to talk about her that way! Especially while she was in earshot!

She wanted to walk out right then and there and quit the circle, but their membership was something Elizabeth absolutely refused to budge on, and she insisted that Rachel attend with her.

"Pay them no never mind," she said, dismissing Rachel's concerns and patting her on the hand. Attend they would, for Pastor Jacob and Elizabeth Templeton's ward was expected to learn the ways of polite society.

Other than the Ladies' Sewing Circle, thank goodness Ransom had spared her much of it!

It didn't take a brilliant scholar to figure out early on that Rachel was different from Wellington's residents.

Raised in almost total seclusion in a log cabin with her father and mother on a farm in the western part of the county, it was obvious that her blustery pa's influence on her had been greater than her gentle mother's.

Outdoors was where she wanted to be, farming the land, hunting and fishing. She preferred trousers to frocks and a rifle to a cooking pot. When compared to the young debutantes of the town, she was quietly labeled by their mothers as nearly hopeless.

Only God could have ordained a husband such as Ransom for her. He was the catch of the town. He could have had his pick of any of Wellington's young ladies. But it was her he wanted. Yes, he wanted her—with all her free-spirited and unworldly ways.

Ransom had saved her. As incredible as it sounded, she believed it to be true. After her mother died, her father signed her over to the care of Jacob and Elizabeth Templeton, and promptly left for Kentucky, leaving her feeling hopeless, scared, abandoned, and alone. They were strangers to her...all of Wellington. But Jacob's youngest son Ransom had stepped in and rescued her from complete emotional wreckage. He had been Rachel's refuge and safety, shielding her, protecting her. He even led her to Christ and eventually married her.

Rachel owed Ransom everything, and her love and commitment to their marriage would remain true as she'd vowed during their recent marriage ceremony.

With this ring I thee wed…with my body I thee worship.

She knew she should try harder to fit in and, with swift resolution, figured now was a good time as any to start.

Holding Ransom's shirt, Rachel was tempted to caress the cloth against her cheek and would have done so if the other ladies hadn't been there.

Instead, Rachel resumed mending his shirt, taking care to make the stitches smaller and more even.

Glancing at her stitching, "Much better, Rachel," Elizabeth commented with a smile.

∞∞∞∞∞∞∞∞∞∞∞∞∞∞∞∞∞

She had never thought of herself as a quitter, so it was a determined Rachel Templeton who insisted to herself, that leaving Wellington, Virginia was not, in fact, quitting, but rather moving on to something better, which was Green River Country in Kentucky.

She had been a strong person, or considered herself to be, and she didn't want anyone to think otherwise. So—keeping things to herself—her doubts and fears—had become second nature, and it would take a very perceptive person to crack open the door to her innermost thoughts.

Rachel had struggled this past year with feelings of rejection…rejection that plagued her at unexpected moments. The overt snubbing by some of Wellington's leading citizens played havoc with her emotions, and if not for the love of her new husband Ransom, she doubted the odds of her survival in this town.

Moreover, and much to her dismay, there had been no word from her father John Winslow since he'd left her to the care of the Templeton family over a year ago. She'd often wondered where he was and if he was still alive in the dark and bloody land of Kentucky. And now, due to unexpected circumstances, the Templeton family and many of Wellington's other residents were moving there as well.

If she left now, would he know where to find her? Surely, someone would tell him where she'd gone…even her most ardent enemies would do that much, or so she hoped.

Rachel's heart skipped a beat as she imagined every conceivable scenario. Perhaps she would meet him again in Kentucky. What would he say? What would he do? When she came face to face with him, would he feel the same as when he walked out of her life on that unforgettable day at the church picnic? Or would he hold his arms out to her, embrace her, and hold her tight? She pictured him—tall, broad-shouldered, black hair and dark eyes. She had been the light of his life at one time, his shadow. Her eyes glistened with tears. Oh! How she missed him so!

CHAPTER TWO

IT HAD RAINED FOR THREE DAYS AND NIGHTS and the river that ran past the northern perimeter of the town overflowed its banks, swelling the streams, inching quickly toward the town of Wellington.

Citing the rain, Ransom had once again refused when Rachel begged to accompany him to the mill this morning.

Upstairs in their bedroom were trunks, their lids open, awaiting Rachel's decision—what to send on the Ohio River, what to take on the journey to Kentucky, and what to leave behind. She sorted and resorted through their belongings, making neat piles on the bed.

Now, in early afternoon, the rain finally stopped and the hot August sun slanted through the shutters as the temperature rose to ninety-nine degrees.

Straightening her back and wiping the back of her hand across her moist forehead, her eyes rested on her mother's portrait on the dressing table.

Had it been nearly two years since Mother died? So many memories rushed at her as she remembered the farm. Of course, no crops were planted this year with Pa gone and the livestock sold when he left.

But happy years were spent there with its inviting cool springs and dense woods. The row of apple trees that lined the lane to the corral, the roses, colorful against the weathered cabin, and walking the fields with Pa.

In spite of the busyness this past year living in Wellington, it lived in her mind ever vividly. Closing her eyes, she remembered again the sound of the wind in the grass and trees, the running water, the smell of dust and pines.

She remembered a place unpeopled and still, unlike the city she was now forced to live in. With a deep sigh, Rachel clutched a dress to her.

From outside, she heard sounds of horses' hooves and creaking carriage wheels and knew the residents were stirring about. Crossing to the window, she opened the shutters and peered out. She desperately needed to get out of the house. But where would she go and, for that matter, what would she tell Jacob and Elizabeth?

She leaned on the sill, watching and listening, and suddenly knew where she was going, knew for the past three days where she was going. The only place. Home! To the farm!

Rachel frowned. But it was sold. She hesitated a moment. A visit…just for a visit…that's all. She could go just for a little while.

Her mind made up, she turned and threw the garment in her hand on the bed. She would not stay indoors another moment!

Quickly brushing her hair before the mirror and slipping on her shoes, she then tread softly down the stairs and escaped the shadowy halls of the house, while Ransom's parents chattered in the kitchen and packed kitchenware into crates.

Rachel hated sneaking out like this, but if she had to stay cooped up one more day packing for the trip, she would absolutely scream!

Once outside, she stepped off the boardwalk, closed her eyes, and turned her face into the sun that blazed down from a hot and copper sky. Though it was scorching, the sun's warmth made her feel like an escapee from the town's jail.

Gus, at the livery stable, would loan her a horse to ride, as he had so often before. But the livery was at the opposite end of town from the parsonage.

No matter. She wanted to get out of Wellington. Somewhere on the farm where she could find a grove of trees to sit under, catch a breeze, and breathe some fresh air, away from the smell of this town. That is, if she could get past the flood that Ransom talked about.

Rachel started toward the heart of town and the closer she got to its center, the larger the crowd became.

Wellington was buzzing like old Charlie Winter's beehives on the outskirts of town, alive and noisy, as residents, housebound during the recent long bout of rain, left their sweltering houses, seeking some relief from the heat.

Horses, some with empty packsaddles, and some carrying everything from furniture to corn in the process of being transported somewhere, crowded the avenue. Many were preparing to depart Wellington for Kentucky, selling what they could, while buying necessary provisions for the trip.

The steamy, humid day turned the town folk into a sweaty, irritable lot as they trudged through the sucking muck, while carriages and wagons maneuvered in and out of the mud holes on Main Street.

"Heaven forbid, that you should stand in line like the rest of us!" a disgruntled customer accused a man who had barged ahead to the front of the crowd at Campbell's Store. Seeing an uprising was about to ensue, he quietly turned and took his place at the end of a line of patrons with perspiration soaked through their clothes, as the sweltering day wore on.

After haggling over the dwindling number of supplies, the townspeople rushed from the stores with their purchases—some gloating over their bargaining skills, and others, disheartened at not as gifted at such cleverness, but thankful they got what they needed. One and all, they hastily loaded their provisions onto the backs of horses or into wagons and buggies.

Rachel pushed by the crowd and when she approached the livery at the edge of town, she stopped in amazement.

Behind it sprawled corrals, some temporary, and outbuildings, and it was busier than she had ever seen. Horses and cattle crowded the pens and transitory enclosures. Tents had been erected, and people were camped about the livery, waiting for the day to leave for Kentucky. Clotheslines had been strung and newly-washed clothes hung over them as children darted around tents, amusing themselves with a game of tag, paying no one any special mind.

"I guess now's not the best time to ask Gus for a horse," she fretted quietly, yet found her feet moving toward Gus again.

Some faces she recognized from church, and to those she nodded. Others were unfamiliar to her.

"Strangers," she muttered softly, "from the county, I suppose."

One stranger, in particular, caught her eye.

A red-haired man.

A very tall, wide-shouldered, red-haired man.

Standing in the shadow of the stable, hat in hand and holding the reins of his horses, it was obvious he was negotiating with Gus.

Gus shrugged his shoulders, threw up his hands and waved them at the encampment, and shook his head "no".

The stranger, clearly disappointed, turned his head away and his eyes lit on Rachel.

Rachel caught her breath and stopped again.

She'd never seen eyes that color.

Nor that intense.

Dancing, cornflower-blue eyes.

The color of the weeds in bloom at this time of year.

Elizabeth's oft-repeated rule of etiquette shot through her mind.

Never look a gentleman directly in the eye.

Yet…something was pulling at her emotions in a way she couldn't fathom…something unfamiliar, rousing her senses in a way never before felt.

Everything within her signaled retreat.

Finding it hard to look away, she went completely still.

A sudden breeze kicked up, blowing gently against her face, and stirred her hair. The wind shifted the shadows of the trees by the livery, but Rachel didn't notice.

A flicker of interest lighting his eyes, the stranger flashed a smile at her and studied her with utter assurance.

Without smiling back, she drew back a step and stared at him as a little flicker of excitement went through her. There was something about him.

"What is it?" she asked herself. "He's not handsomer than other men I know, so it can't be his looks."

But there was something big and sure about him, something in his stance, or something from inside of him. He was a man that knew himself, knew his strength and his weakness and had come to terms with who he was.

All of that, she instinctively knew with one glance.

"Rachel?" asked a harried Gus, raking a hand through his hair. "Is there something I can do for you?"

"Uh—uh, no," Rachel stammered. "Thanks, Gus," she answered in a rush, as she tried again to pull her eyes away from the red-haired stranger.

She wished now that she had not come.

Wished she had not left the house.

Wished this man didn't unsettle her so.

Eyes twinkling at her obvious discomfiture, the stranger placed his hat on his head, and pulled his smile wider.

How dare he look at me in such a way!

Color high and her dark hair tossing in the wind, Rachel turned swiftly and walked away, fighting down an overwhelming urge to run, to get away, somewhere, anywhere, away from this feeling.

Away from this man.

She was tempted to turn around for one last look as she felt his gaze follow her down the street, but felt too distraught to do so.

Home! She needed to get home!

CHAPTER THREE

PROSPERITY HAD FLOURISHED IN WELLINGTON as it had in eastern Virginia, changing the landscape of untamed wilderness to one of music, books, and the arts.

However, a restlessness lying beneath the surface of Wellington's male settlers was apparent as talk at their frequent male gatherings often turned to past escapades of danger and uncertainty. A part of them longed for adventure and they secretly scorned the tameness and predictability of life in Wellington.

When Reverend Templeton, pastor of the largest church in town, announced he was relocating to Kentucky, enthusiasm spread like wildfire as these restless men envisioned new territory to conquer.

Needless to say, some of their wives were less than eager to leave the comfortable homes and community they had become accustomed to, with its endless socials and committees. They did not want to abandon faithful and long-time friends; and above all, some of their own children, who had married and settled nearby. The crying and hand-wringing of these despairing women did not persuade many of the men to change their minds. So in the end, reluctantly, and in some cases with considerable bitterness, their wives made plans to leave.

Twenty-year-old Ransom Templeton was striding briskly down the walk as men from the county loitered on benches or leaned lazily against walls, curiously watching wagons and buggies pass by, driven by men with tension etched on their faces. The youngest of Pastor Jacob Templeton's three sons, Ransom had an easy way about him that found some affinity with all, young or old. And having grown up in Wellington, he knew, and was known by, everyone.

"Ransom!" called Gerald Miller through the open door as Ransom passed by the long, narrow, tonsorial parlor.

Ransom stopped and stepped inside the shop, removing his hat.

"Hello, Mr. Miller!" he answered.

Glancing at Ransom's hair tied back in a queue, he asked, "Need a haircut, Ransom?" Gerald knew that he didn't since he'd been in a few days ago for a trim, but business was slow and since so much of the town was preparing to leave for Kentucky, he felt a little woe-be-gone at being left behind.

"No, thanks, Mr. Miller," Ransom said. "We're packing up and getting ready to leave for Kentucky."

"Yes, yes. I'm sure sorry to see you go, boy," Mr. Miller said, his face a little crestfallen. "We're going to miss you around here."

Ransom had tried a few days ago to talk Mr. Miller in coming with them. "Come with us," Ransom urged again.

Shaking his head, Mr. Miller answered, "Martha's been talking about going but—"

Shrugging his shoulders, he said, "I don't know about that. I think I'm getting too old to make a new start." With a gleam in his eyes, he joked, "Besides—where would people here get another barber?"

"Well, look at it this way," Ransom reasoned, "I don't think there'll be many folk left when we leave."

"You may be right about that." Crossing his arms, he absently studied the floor. "Hmm… how would I ever get my goods and equipment there?"

"There's a big shipment headed down the Ohio when we leave. Will would be the best person to talk to about that." Ransom placed his hand on Gerald's shoulder for a moment.

"I just want to tell you, Mr. Miller, you were one of the few that stuck by me a year ago when the church board wanted to crucify Rachel and my family. I want you to know that I'll never forget that. You find out who your real friends are in tough times," Ransom admitted.

Mr. Miller was a rather short man, portly, with thinning gray hair. He looked up at Ransom's towering face and with the faintest hint of a smile, said, "I've known you your whole life, Ransom. You've always shown yourself to be a sincere and honest person. And getting to know Rachel this past year, I've found the same to be true of her."

"A shame some of the others can't see that," Ransom said with a hint of irritation in his voice. "I realize Rachel's different in some ways but she wasn't raised in the city. Her father and mother kept her pretty secluded for most of her young life. She doesn't see the world as some of us do."

With a grin, he said, "Pretty much a free spirit."

Gerald Miller chuckled at that. Attractive as Rachel was, she had never become pretentious about her looks. She'd gone against society, for certain, when she wore trousers on occasion. She also refused to wear a cap as the other women did. Free spirit? He supposed so.

Martha had once whispered to him, her eyes darting around at anyone that might overhear, that Elizabeth Templeton had confided she had a difficult time getting Rachel to wear a corset. That bit of information brought a chuckle as he envisioned the stand-off between those two head-strong females.

And then, there was that business of her marrying a gambler and him divorcing her. The town was still in an uproar about that. But as far as he could tell it wasn't her fault. Anyway, far be it from him to judge her.

"Could be, Ransom," said Mr. Miller. "Though, I might be more inclined to consider her naïve."

Throwing up his hands, he said, "However, free spirit or not, it was the least that I could do when I spoke up for you at that church meeting."

"Just the same, thanks." Ransom shifted his feet, peering out the door, anxious to leave. Having worked hard all morning, he wanted to stop at the inn for a bite to eat.

Placing his hand on Mr. Miller's arm, "Do consider coming with us," he insisted gently. "I know Father would be pleased."

"I will…I will," Gerald said with a wave of his hand. "I'll talk to Martha about it some more this very night."

"Great! Sorry to go, but I've got to run." Looking back over his shoulder, Ransom called, "Hope to see you in the party when we leave."

Stepping out the door, he put his hat back on and, with a soft whistle, continued his brisk stepping down the gray, silvery boards of the walk.

He'd always liked Mr. Miller. Not only had Gerald Miller been the town's barber for many years, but a Bible scholar as well. Over the years, many pleasant conversations had taken place between them as they studied and debated doctrine.

Having lived in Wellington since he was a young man, change was not something that came easy for Gerald Miller. The pioneer spirit was nothing he had ever aspired to, although his father's and grandfather's stories about their adventures and antics in earlier years, had fascinated him as a lad.

His privileged childhood on their plantation along a deep tidal river in Virginia seemed such a long time ago. Their plantation had its own wharf, and often ocean-going ships coming from England, would drop anchor and drop off necessities and every luxury you could think of.

Not wanting to be separated from his family, he had reluctantly embarked from their own dock for schooling in England. Unexpectedly, a short time later, he had been summoned home because of the untimely death of his mother. Eventually, the family's grand lifestyle that included dances in the plantation ballroom, and men and women dressed in the latest London fashions, resumed, along with horse-races, betting, card games, and musicales.

But trouble loomed on the horizon. His grandfather was in debt to the British trading houses, and eventually as overproduction of poorly-produced tobacco in the Tidewater resulted in the drop of price of tobacco, he lost everything. His plantation, wealth, and opulent lifestyle were gone!

Moving from the Tidewater coastal plain and then further west across the Piedmont in Virginia, Gerald's family was among a few other plantation owners that had lost their fortunes. They never regained the wealth or lifestyle they once had, but made a decent living raising corn. His grandfather and father remained undaunted by their losses of the past, for they reveled in change.

But, for Gerald as a boy, this did nothing for him but instill a longing for the security of putting down roots.

And now, many of the people he had grown to know so well, were pulling out of Wellington. It felt as though his family was leaving him and while part of him wanted to stay, the other part wanted to stick with family, no matter where they went.

"Yes…." he said thoughtfully, resigning himself to the situation at hand. "I suppose I could move…one last time."

CHAPTER FOUR

"RANSOM! RANSOM TEMPLETON!"

Above the din of the crowd, Ransom heard his name called, and turned in the direction of the voice.

Narrowing his eyes against the glare of the hot afternoon sun and craning his neck, he scanned the crowd on the shaded walk across the street until he spotted a shock of red hair.

Shading his face with his hand, Ransom saw Sam Spencer, his friend from the university, waving from across the street.

A smile lit his face. "Sam!" Ransom yelled and motioned with his hand. "Come across!"

Avoiding a wagon drawn by a team of horses that jolted by, and sidestepping a deep puddle, Sam's long legs bounded across the muddied street, leading his horses. Securing them at the rail, he stepped onto the walk and the two men locked forearms for a few seconds.

Both men were tall, well over six feet, but as different in looks as they were in personality. Ransom had hazel eyes and auburn hair, was soft-spoken and reserved, while Sam possessed blue eyes, flame-red hair, and a personality that was energetic and quick of wit.

"Good to see you, Sam!" Grinning impishly while hooking his thumbs in his waistband, he said, "I was wondering if you'd really come."

"You doubted me?" Sam asked, with a look of mock disapproval. "I told you, Ransom, my mind's made up. I'm going to Kentucky."

Ransom nodded. "Well, there was quite a spell there that you were trying to decide whether you wanted to practice law or go to Kentucky as a minister."

The crowded walk forced the two men to step aside as some rambunctious boys accidently plowed into Sam. He put his hands on an offending boy's shoulders and gently pushed him away.

"Well," Sam said with finality, "I've decided that I can do both in Kentucky."

"Good decision!" Ransom said. "When did you get into Wellington? This morning?"

Sam took off his hat and, pulling a handkerchief from his pocket, wiped his forehead.

"About an hour ago. I took my horses to the livery, but it's like a madhouse there. It seems everyone and their relatives have their livestock boarded there."

He repositioned the hat on his head, tucked his handkerchief in his pocket, and looked around, his eyes missing nothing. "Seems like the whole town is in an uproar, with all these comings and goings."

"Uproar is the word, all right," Ransom agreed, following Sam's gaze.

"Is the whole town going with us?"

Ransom smiled. "Not quite...but Father figures about two hundred."

Ransom lowered his head in thought for a moment, and then said, "We'll take your horses home and stable them in our barn. They're probably safer there, anyway."

Sam nodded in agreement.

"My guess is, you're starved. So…what say we get a bite at the inn after that? I was just on my way over there, as a matter of fact."

"Sounds good to me." He moved off the walk, untied the horses, and stepped into the saddle. "Lead the way."

"By the way," said Ransom as he started off, "Tom McClelland arrived in town a couple of days ago. He's staying at the inn. We'll look him up while we're there."

∞∞∞∞∞∞∞∞∞∞∞∞∞∞∞

Ransom and Sam stomped their boots on the back stoop of the parsonage, loosening the clods of mud that clung to them. Jacob and Elizabeth were busily packing cooking pots and utensils into wooden crates standing in the middle of the kitchen.

The day was hot and flies came in the open windows, huge flies that drove a body to distraction as constant, futile swiping did not discourage them from settling on flesh.

Elizabeth looked up as the men came through the door and quickly swept back a lock of her hair that had escaped its cap. The men removed their hats and with a flip of the wrist, Ransom sailed his hat onto the table and introduced Sam to his parents.

"Father, Mother. This is my friend from the university, Sam Spencer. Sam, these are my parents, Jacob and Elizabeth Templeton."

Shaking hands, Jacob said, "It's good to finally meet you, Sam. Ransom has told us so much about you."

"Good to meet you, sir."

Using his hat, Sam whipped the dust from his pants and immediately regretted it, for the dirt filled the air in the kitchen. He quickly stole a look at Elizabeth's face.

"Pardon my appearance," he said sheepishly, "but I rode for several days to get here."

"You just got into town, Mr. Spencer?" asked Elizabeth.

"Yes, ma'am," he answered, "this very day, in fact."

Turning toward the stove, she said, "Let me fix you something to eat, then."

Ransom caught his mother's arm. "No, thanks, Mother, just the same."

Wiping the back of his hand across his forehead, he said, "It's too miserably hot to cook. We just stopped by to drop off Sam's horses at our barn. Everything's crazy in town and the livery is overflowing with, not just animals, but people. Sam and I are going to the inn and look up Tom McClelland. We'll grab a bite while we're there."

"Now, Ransom, you know I don't mind," Elizabeth protested, already bending over a crate searching for the necessary utensils. "It won't take long to rustle something together."

"Yes, I know, Mother, but *I* mind," he said, placing his hand over hers. "You're busy with all this packing."

At that moment, Rachel walked into the kitchen and gave a small start. Her hand stopped swishing her painted fan as she looked into cornflower-blue eyes for the second time that day.

His hat in his hand, Sam made no move toward her, not even the perfunctory bow. He stood, a smile beginning to draw his lips, his eyes fixed on her, and Rachel struggled to focus her eyes on something else—anything else.

Humiliation brought heat to her face as she remembered their meeting today. What must he think of her now? No lady ever stared at a man in such a way! She was chaste, but had acted otherwise, and the memory shamed her to her toes.

What kind of woman was she, a married woman, to be thinking like this of any other man? It was wrong. It was all wrong. She should not feel this way.

She could not resist turning to him again.

Oh, those eyes! A grin creeping into them, they were looking at her and seemed to stare right into her confused thoughts. Rachel leaned toward Ransom, wishing she could disappear completely.

"Sam," Ransom said, drawing her to him. "I'd like you to meet Rachel…my wife."

Wife!

"We were married a few weeks ago," he added.

Sam's smile slowly faded at the girl in the crook of Ransom's arm.

The girl at the livery who turned and ran like a scared rabbit at his smile!

Ransom's *wife*!

He regarded her with studied intent, taking in the black hair and eyes to match, his eyes lingering on her hands as they nervously twisted the fan.

Never in all of his talk about Rachel at the university did Ransom convey the beauty that stood before him now. The wavy hair flowing down her back would have looked childish on someone else, but on her it was simply elegant. He doubted that the most gifted artist could paint a portrait that would do her justice.

Sam was never at a loss for words, but he was now.

There she was…all any man could want. Ransom's wife…she was *his*.

Ransom's arm about her brought Sam a sharp twinge of jealousy that surprised him. He never felt that way about any girl, for they had meant little to him in the past.

Sensing that all eyes turned on him, waiting for his reply, Sam quickly composed himself, nodded toward her, and exclaimed, "So! This is Rachel. I heard a lot about you at the university. I must say," he paused, a touch of awe coloring his voice, "everything Ransom told me about you was true…and then some."

Rachel's eyes opened wide and, as a blush inflamed her cheeks again, she turned to look at Ransom. "Ransom talked about me?"

Laughing, Sam said, "You were often his main topic of conversation."

Sobering, his smile softened. "He said you were beautiful and I must say, I agree with him."

Ransom's chuckle was dry. "Watch him, Rachel," he cautioned. "Sam can be quite a ladies' man in spite of that head of red hair."

Sam looked at Ransom quickly. Did Ransom detect what he was feeling? No, he decided, he didn't think so.

Suddenly, with a twist of an imaginary mustache, and a burlesque half-bow, Sam looked again at Rachel and said, "Fear not, Madam Templeton. As you are the wife of one of my best friends, I assure you, dear lady, you are safe with me, and I shall guard you with my life."

Rachel tried hard to smile as the family broke into laughter, but looked as though she had swallowed a handful of gnats.

"It's good to know that someone who has a good sense of humor will be traveling with us," said Elizabeth. "We're going to need all the humor we can get," she said, a thread of concern in her voice.

"There's no sense doing all this worrying, Elizabeth," said Jacob as he frowned at her. "God has everything in His hands."

"I know, I know." She shook her head and threw up her hands. "But we've been so accustomed to comfortably living here with very few real problems."

"I understand that." Jacob studied her a moment. "If you still have reservations about this, Elizabeth, now's the time to let me know."

Elizabeth bit the inside of her cheek as she fought back the dark thoughts plucking at her mind. "No. No. You're right, Jacob," she waved a hand in his direction. "I worry too much. God *does* have things in His hands."

Elizabeth's mood was contagious and gloom settled over the room. Ransom didn't like the puckered look on his mother's face...didn't like it at all. He'd been so excited about moving to Kentucky and didn't want to start on this journey spooked by her.

Ransom shook himself slightly and retrieved his hat from the table.

"Yes, and with that said, Sam and I will be going to the inn. I'll be back later."

Sam gave a tip of his hat. "It's been a delight, Mrs. Templeton."

Then turning to Rachel, "*And,* Mrs. Templeton."

CHAPTER FIVE

THE INN WAS A PLEASANT SURPRISE TO SAM. The red and gold window tapestries, reflected in the elaborate mirrors hanging in the dining area, gave the feeling that one was dining in a large city, instead of the moderate town of Wellington.

He relaxed in the atmosphere after his ride of several days. He was unshaven and his jaws itched under the stubble. He was dirty, and he was a man who liked to be clean.

They gave their food order to the waiter. As the waiter walked away, Ransom folded his arms, elbows on the table, and leaned in towards Sam.

"So…where are you staying until we leave, Sam?"

"Got a room at the inn here, actually," he said as he looked around at the crowd, "and it wasn't easy. This town is crowded."

Sam rubbed his bristly face. "I could stand a shave and a good soak in a tub right now."

"Why don't you stay at the parsonage with us?" Ransom asked. "I know everything is chaotic at the present, but I'm sure Mother wouldn't mind."

Sam shook his head. "Thanks, anyway, Ransom. But I saw how everything is packed up there." He shrugged his shoulders. "And it's just a few more days before we leave. Besides, I've business to attend to. I've made arrangements to buy some cattle for the trip."

Sam's mind drifted to Rachel, and he leaned back in his chair, studying Ransom. With a contrived air of indifference, he remarked, "I must say, old friend, I am surprised to hear you married Rachel. I know you had doubts about her while at the university." Rubbing his hand over the tablecloth, he asked, "What happened to change your mind?"

Ransom smiled sheepishly. "I finally realized that she was the one that God had picked out for me."

"Really!" Sam exclaimed. "How so?" he asked, his interest piqued.

"Well…you know I spent a lot of time in prayer about it. It just seemed that was the way God was working things out."

He raised his hand and shook his head as Sam attempted to contradict his answer. "I know, I know. I didn't think she would fit into the lifestyle of being a minister's wife. She's so independent and, in some ways, unconventional. But I finally saw that," he grasped for words as his hand swiped the air, "her…um…earthiness made her exactly the kind of wife I needed in relocating to Kentucky…you know, a wilderness bride. Plus, I finally accepted what my heart knew the first time I saw her, that I loved her."

Ransom paused and the smile left his face. "Sam, I'm going to tell you some things that have happened to Rachel. And since you'll probably hear them from someone on the journey, 'tis better you hear them from me first."

The waiter brought coffee and hot rolls, interrupting their conversation. "Can I get anything else for you gentlemen while you're waiting for your order?"

Ransom said, "No thanks, Frank."

"Right."

As Frank was turning away, Ransom asked, "By the way, Frank, how's your wife, Louise?"

"Oh, she's all right, Ransom, but she's in quite a state, wanting to leave with the other folk to Kentucky. You know, she sets quite a store by your mother Elizabeth. We hate to see the Templeton family pull up stakes and leave, not only the church, but, this town. We're going to miss your father as our pastor."

Frank shrugged his shoulders. "But, I told Louise maybe the next go-round. We've got a little money saved, but not enough to buy supplies *and* land." He grinned and with a wink, he joked, "Perhaps that will give her enough incentive to stay out of the shops."

Ransom gave a little laugh. "You may be right, Frank. Listen, excuse my rudeness. I forgot to introduce you to my friend, Sam Spencer." Ransom bobbed his head toward Frank. "Sam, meet Frank Morgan, a local resident and good friend of mine."

Sam nodded.

"Sam was a student with me at the university. He's going as a missionary minister to Kentucky, too, and since he studied law, will also set up office as an attorney."

Frank smiled. "Well, God speed to you both. Noble work you're doing, and I wish you both a safe journey. I've heard it's pretty dangerous."

Ransom rubbed his chin. "Yes, that's what I understand. But, fortunately, many of the folks from town have decided to not let that stop them from going. Even Doctor Stone has agreed to go with us. He said since many of the young families are leaving town, he'd better be on hand to deliver all the babies they will have.

"The organization has given us the mandate to start churches and set up schools in the Green River Country of Kentucky. It's an exciting time, for sure."

Ransom raked his thumbnail against the side of his mouth thoughtfully. "Listen, Frank," he said. "I'm going to need some help on my land in Kentucky. Why don't you and Louise consider coming with us and working for me? I can't pay much right now, but I'll give you a share of the profits from the crops and sale of livestock. That should get you enough to purchase some land for yourself. That's what several families are doing."

Frank's mouth dropped open. "Seriously? You're asking us to go with you, Ransom?"

"Sure." Ransom smiled. "Think that's something you'd want to do?"

"Would I!" he exclaimed. "How soon before we leave?"

"We're waiting for the scout to show up in town. I'd say in a couple or three days. Think you can be ready by then?"

Frank's mind was in a whirl. Thinking of the preparations it would take to leave, he shifted excitedly from one foot to the other. This was what he had dreamed of doing. He wasn't raised to be a town-dweller and longed to be back in farming. He'd been earnestly praying that God would make a way, and here, when he least expected, the door was opened for him.

"I'll be ready. I'll go tell the boss this is my last day." He laid his hand on Ransom's shoulder. "Thanks, Ransom. You don't know how much this means to Louise and me."

Ransom waved his hand. "You're doing *me* a favor, Frank, by going. To tell you the truth," Ransom gave a short laugh as he shook his head, "Rachel's not the best cook in the world. Maybe Louise could give her some pointers."

Frank agreed enthusiastically. "That she can do. You know, Louise is just about the best cook around." He looked toward the kitchen. "If you'll excuse me, the inn is bustling today and my boss is giving me the evil eye. I've got to get back to work." Nodding to Sam, he said, "Pleased to make your acquaintance, Mr. Spencer."

"Good man, that Frank," said Ransom as Frank walked away.

"So…you were going to enlighten me to some dark secrets about Rachel?"

"No dark secrets," Ransom cleared his throat. "Well, that's not completely true. But there are   some sad events that happened to her."

Sam waited for Ransom to continue. He wasn't into idle gossip, but he *was* curious about *her.*

Ransom considered what he was about to say for a long moment before he actually came out with it. He felt a little bit like a tale-bearer, but he'd got to know Sam well enough at the university to know that Sam could be trusted.

"Do you remember at the university," he finally replied, "that I told you after Rachel's mother died, her father made my father custodian over her and the farm her father deeded to her?"

Sam nodded.

Ransom took a sip of his coffee and absent-mindedly rearranged his silverware and his eyes flashed with a rare bit of temper.

"While I was gone to university, Rachel met a man by the name of Peter Brogade.

"In October, he charmed her into marrying him without revealing his true intentions, which were to sell her farm and take the proceeds to do some high-stakes gambling. He was abusive toward her, but she refused to sell. She left him and moved back into the parsonage with Father and Mother.

"What Peter didn't know, was that Rachel's father had given Father full control over the farm, even if she was married. When Peter found he couldn't use marital rights as the basis for selling the farm, he left Wellington in December. In January, Rachel discovered she was pregnant with Peter's baby. She wouldn't tell my parents about her pregnancy and, in March, she moved back to the farm."

"Didn't your parents object?"

"Sure," he answered with a shrug. "They tried their best to talk her out of it. However, she was legally married and there wasn't much they could do to stop her. She was due to have the baby in July. When I arrived home in May and discovered where she was, I, immediately, went to the farm. When I got there, she was seven months pregnant and in labor."

Ransom rubbed his hand over the nape of his neck. "I delivered Rachel's baby. The baby was still-born."

Except for a thoughtful blink of his eyes, Sam gave no response.

"My parents have never known about her pregnancy...or if they did, they've never let on. Anyway, I brought Rachel back to the parsonage to recover." Ransom paused, thinking back to that day. "About the last of June, she received a post informing her that Peter had divorced her. He never knew about the baby."

Something flickered across Sam's face as his brows drew into a slight frown. Ransom caught the look and immediately came to Rachel's defense.

"Sam, don't judge her for this," he said, irritably. I know divorce is practically unheard of, and I realize a divorced woman becomes the talk of society, but you'd have to know Rachel. She's absolutely innocent in all of this, except possibly, one bad judgment."

"True," Sam was thinking, "divorced people are under the ban of social society. Strange that someone like Ransom would throw off all constraint and oppose tradition. The views and principles of others have always been such a part of his decision making."

As for Sam…the opinions of others mattered little.

Sam smiled a reassuring smile and said, "I'm not judging her. After all, Saint Paul said if the unbelieving wish to depart…let them depart, and that the Christian is not under bondage.

"I was just thinking that she's so young to have gone through so much."

Picking up his cup, he asked, "How old is she now, anyway?"

"She'll be seventeen in a couple of days. I was there when she got Peter's post, and I immediately asked her to marry me. We were married a week later. Of course, some of the people have been in a fury over it."

Sam sat quietly in thought, while staring into his cup as though an answer lay in its bottom to the questions in his mind.

Questions he should not ask...had no right to.

Yet…he wanted—no—needed an answer.

He hesitated and then asked casually, "I know it's none of my business, Ransom, but does Rachel love you?"

Startled that Sam posed such an intimate question, Ransom did not answer right away.

"She says she does," Ransom finally said.

"Sam," he added, "I love her with all my heart."

Sam looked straight at him and smiled. "I've always known that. She's got a good man."

Ransom picked up a roll, and slathered butter on it. "More importantly, I've got a good woman."

He bit into the roll, chewed quickly, and swallowed.

"To tell you the truth…sometimes I'm riddled with guilt. I never mentioned my feelings to her before I left for the university. I watched over her and protected her while I was with her, but I never really courted her. Will tried to warn me that someone would come along and steal her away for he knew I was in love with her. He was right, of course, but I wouldn't listen. Thinking there was plenty of time to win her love, I procrastinated until his prediction finally came true. I'm partly to blame in all of this."

Sam was quiet. He would have pursued a different tack. Courting Rachel would have been an easy decision for him…should he have wanted to.

With a shrug, he replied, "Forget it, Ransom. That's all in the past. You must look to the future and all it holds."

"You don't understand, Sam. Her divorce can't be swept under the rug. It is part and parcel of her life now—" pausing for a few seconds, he added, "and mine."

Sam brows drew together again and he peered sharply at Ransom's face. "Is that regret I'm hearing, Ransom?" he questioned.

Ransom hesitated. "No…no of course not," he stammered.

Sam wasn't convinced. It took Ransom a little too long to answer.

"No," Ransom reiterated. "Just struggling with my own thoughts, that's all."

Sam's brow crinkled again. It wasn't hard to figure out that Rachel didn't meet Ransom's expectation of perfection. "A normal wife she is not" he had said. There was no doubt, whatsoever, that Ransom loved her, but his strong conviction of what a minister's wife should be like, caused him to overlook the jewel he suspected she really was.

"Perhaps you don't love her as much as you think," Sam commented blatantly.

"Now really…Sam," Ransom said, bristling. "Rachel's the love of my life. I've never met anyone quite like her. She stole my heart from first glance. Honestly, I don't know what I would do without her. I wasn't looking for anyone to fall in love with when she walked into my life. God only knows how hard I fought the feelings I had for her. It hit me the first time I laid eyes on her. I haven't even considered anyone else since that day. I didn't think it possible that anyone could wrap around my heart like she has."

Sam had hit a nerve. Better to leave well enough alone. He'd meant no harm. He always tended to be blunt when commenting, and he expected the same from others in return. But often he found that was something others could neither easily take nor give. Ransom's friendship mattered a great deal to him and he didn't want to lose it.

"Well," Sam smiled encouragingly, "perhaps the change in scenery will alleviate some of the questions in your mind."

"Maybe so," Ransom pondered out loud.

Sam leaned back in his chair again. "How is Rachel emotionally?" Sam asked. "Has she been able to work through all of this?"

"That's the hard part. She doesn't realize it, but she is still suffering. Rejection has hit her hard. Sometimes she feels people are against her and…" laying down his knife, he sighed, "sad to say at times her feelings are correct. I think she blames herself for the death of her baby."

Ransom lowered his voice a shade. "She made the wrong choice when she married Peter and she feels she is reaping what she sowed."

Looking at Sam, Ransom went on, "Of course, you know as well as I do that, people give a divorced woman a hard time, even if it's not her fault. She's a good person and I feel people attack her unjustly."

"Makes you want to put on your shining armor and defend her, doesn't it?" Sam grinned as his words conjured up knights jostling for the honor of fair maidens.

A frown burrowed Ransom's forehead. "Maybe that's where I fail her." Uncertainty colored his voice. "I'm pretty much a peacemaker and hope that things will work out all right…eventually. So, most of the time, I just hold my peace."

Sam's face took on a thoughtful look. "Hmm…be careful about that, Ransom. Holding your peace doesn't always solve problems. Often it's better to face them and try to bring about some resolution. I know Scripture says 'blessed are the peacemakers', but there's a difference between peacemakers and peacekeepers. Peacekeepers try to keep the peace at any cost, even at the price of compromising principles. Peacemakers try to resolve without compromising. Do you understand what I mean?"

Ransom's brows knit together. "I'm not sure. I'll have to think on that a while."

"Nevertheless, Rachel *is* your wife," Sam said, "and she's entitled to your loyalty."

A twinge of conscience pricked Sam, even as he said that. As sharp as he was about women, Sam had an instinct about Rachel. There was something about her…an undeniable innocence. He wasn't accustomed to girls such as her and felt a sense of envy that Ransom had married her. Growing uncomfortable with his thoughts, Sam shuffled in his chair and decided to change the subject.

"How about the rest of your family? Everyone set for the trip?"

"Some are, some aren't. The family has decided to send most of our furniture and goods down the Ohio River. We've decided not to travel that way ourselves. Even though it's the most dangerous way, the Wilderness Road is the cheapest way to travel. But the Ohio has its dangers too, with Indians waiting on the banks to kill the passengers and take the goods. Besides, it's hard to find experienced men to navigate those waters. My oldest brother Will has decided to have his sawmill and other equipment shipped on the river, too."

"I'm looking forward to meeting Will."

"I probably shouldn't mention it, but Will's wife Jane isn't too keen about leaving her parents behind, and I'm afraid there's been a lot of fussing between them."

He shrugged. "Oh, well, it's really none of my business."

Ransom smiled. "My other brother James, and his wife Cissa, are all set and agreeable with the move though."

Ransom's face brightened. "Hey! I told you Tom McClelland was here. But, I didn't tell you, his older brother Robert and his wife Cordelia are going, too. They have two young children. I believe they said their names were Adam and Starr."

"Is Robert an attorney, too?"

"No. He's into banking. Tom said Robert is carrying quite a bit of gold with him with which he intends to establish a bank in Stone Valley."

"Hmm," Sam said thoughtfully. "He'll need to keep an eye on his money."

"You're right about that."

Frank brought their order and thinking back to his comment about Rachel's birthday, Ransom said, "You know, Rachel didn't have a birthday party last year. Things got all confused. Perhaps Mother can arrange something tomorrow evening. She's an expert at entertaining. You'll come, won't you, Sam? I'll ask Tom and his family, too."

"Sure," Sam answered with unease. "Nothing could keep me away."

CHAPTER SIX

RACHEL'S FACE WAFTED BEFORE SAM as he sat soaking in the tub. Since he'd met her this afternoon, it had been hard to keep her from intruding on his thoughts.

The attraction he felt for her caught him off-guard. She was Ransom's wife and he silently berated himself for what he was thinking.

Sam recalled nights spent with Ransom at the university in front of the fire. Silently scoffing at Ransom's declaration of "love at first sight" for Rachel, he could now understand why Ransom fell for her so easily.

Having been romantically acquainted with many girls in the past, Sam had not believed in such a phenomenon. To him, romance was an amorous game of intrigue, and any girl who set her sights on him, eventually found herself in an unhappy and futile situation, for no girl had been successful in casting a spell over him.

He had known many young ladies, in view of the fact that his father was a congressman in Virginia. The political scene had introduced him to a number of young women, whose life's ambition was to make a suitable match.

His wits, concerning women, were sharp, and Sam saw through them in an instant. Their behavior was only a charade that masked their ambitions to climb the social ladder. He had seen through their schemes and played the game without committing himself to any one girl.

Too bad his father Oliver couldn't see their ambitious designs. But in a way, Sam couldn't blame him. His father had grown tired of his wild ways, getting Sam out of one scrape after another, and he wanted Sam to settle down. After hearing that Sam was heading out for Kentucky, Oliver wondered if this was just another adventure Sam was embarking on and he had as much as said so.

Sam had been a hard nut emotionally since boyhood. He had seen other men reduced to the point of silliness over some girl, but at no time were emotions a driving force in his life. Cold reason had always been the basis for his actions, good or bad. There were few ladies who could resist his charms when he chose to exert them, and he laughed to himself as he remembered he had become known as "Slippery Sam", for he'd slipped right through any girl's plans for all of his twenty-five years.

But after years of the excitement of the chase, he'd grown tired of the phoniness that women thought it was their role to project.

"It isn't their fault," he had concluded a year ago. "They are taught to be that way. There has to be more to life than the vanities it holds."

Ministry had been on his mind this past year, not women.

And now, when he least expected it, feelings came stealing over him like a thief in the night. Feelings, he'd never experienced before and felt unprepared to handle.

He closed his eyes and Rachel's face materialized in his mind as he recalled her dark eyes with long black lashes that curled upward, setting off to perfection her high cheekbones that glowed with a slight tan. Dark tendrils hung loosely around her face and would sway slightly as she swished her fan, trying to cool herself. Nothing had escaped him as he observed sleeves pushed up on slender arms and her hand fumbling with her perspiring neck.

Sam thought back to the long winter evenings spent in front of the fire at the university as Ransom revealed any details he could remember about her. The way she smiled, her stubbornness and independence, her pride and vulnerabilities, and how her dark eyes would turn black when she was angry. In Sam's mind's eye, he saw the dark smoldering that would draw any man in.

Though he had never realized this until now, the long winter evenings in conversation with Ransom had etched Rachel into his own heart, too, and Sam had come to feel he knew her as well as Ransom did.

Sighing in frustration, he knew he would never betray God, or his good friend Ransom. Other men's wives were strictly off limits.

He leaned back in the tub and the corners of his mouth turned down as he relived past relationships in his mind. "Ah…single girls are different." The challenging pursuit, unabashed, flirtatious words spoken on the edge of propriety and the thrill of escape, once he had captured their hearts, had always fulfilled his sense of adventure for the moment. He had taken the feelings of other girls for granted, slipping easily out of their grasp.

Suddenly, he became angrier at himself than he could ever remember being, and struck the water he was sitting in with his fist, sloshing it over the sides of the tub.

Not only was she Ransom's wife, but they were newly married and Ransom was one of his best friends. He had envisioned years of working with Ransom in ministry, but hadn't bargained on Rachel.

He'd always been a cavalier rogue, carelessly brushing aside the tears and broken dreams of girls whose hearts he had casually wounded. He had never needed to guard his own heart before in his relationships, for they had meant nothing to him.

But since becoming a Christian two years ago, he had not as much as kept company with any girl. His mind was set on ministry, and he was a highly disciplined man, always obtaining what he set out for.

Whatsoever a man soweth, that shall he also reap.

"How true!" he said aloud to himself. "My past transgressions have come home to haunt me."

He thought of the long years of enforced silence before him and grimly surmised, "There's only one alternative. Avoid Rachel as much as possible...and pray!

CHAPTER SEVEN

JOHN WINSLOW RODE INTO TOWN, leading four horses behind him with packs laden with supplies on their sides. Fringed moccasins reached all the way up to his knees. A pair of buckskin leggings, the dark blue of a hunter's shirt and a low-crowned felt hat on his head completed his look.

He dismounted in front of the parsonage.

Carrying a package in her arms, Rachel spied him as she was nearing home. Even at that distance, and squinting in the sun, there was no mistaking the physique and stance of her father.

She stopped so suddenly that Ransom jolted into her, sending her package tumbling to the boardwalk. Her hand clasped her throat and she began working her mouth, trying to bring words to her lips, but no sounds came forth. Her face went white and Ransom, thinking she was going to faint, caught her arm. But Rachel threw off his hand and with skirts flying, raced down the street.

"Pa! Pa!"

John Winslow looked up from the reins he was tethering at the rail.

"Rachel!" he called as he stepped towards her. She leapt into his arms, and the burly man lifted her up and swung her around.

"Pa! Oh, Pa!"

"Rachel! I've missed you, girl! Oh, how I've missed you!"

He finally set her on the ground as Ransom came strolling up. She clutched John's arm as Ransom introduced himself as Rachel's husband, the youngest son of Reverend Jacob Templeton.

A look of astonishment passed over John's face. He turned to her. His daughter, to him just a child, was married?

"Husband? You're married now, girl? Jacob Templeton's son?"

He thought about that a long moment. He had hated to leave her like he did, yet now that she was married was a distinct relief to him. His ideas on women were strict and old-fashioned, and he had feared she would take little note of the rules of men.

"Well, now!" he said suddenly, "So much the better. It'll be easier to give my attention to the party as you'll have a husband to look after you."

"What do you mean, Pa?" Rachel asked, puzzled.

"Didn't anyone tell you?" John glanced at Ransom as Ransom tried to stifle a grin. "I'm your guide to Kentucky."

While Rachel's brain was trying to make sense of what he'd just told her, Ransom's eyes twinkled as he watched her.

Rachel turned to Ransom. "Did you know Pa was our guide to Kentucky?" she asked.

Grinning and rocking on his heels, he answered. "Sure did. Thought it might make a good surprise."

"You knew all this time?"

"Yep."

"How could you, Ransom Templeton!" she demanded sharply. "Knowing how much I missed him!"

John Winslow threw back his head and laughed. "Marriage sure hasn't changed you, girl! You've still got a temper."

"So I have, Pa," she admitted, unruffled by his criticism. "I guess I'm just like you."

John threw up his hands. "Hey, wait, Rachel, girl. I've changed a lot. I'm a Christian now for your information," he informed her.

Her eyes opened wide. "You are? A Christian? Oh, Pa, I'm so glad."

Smiling, as though she were revealing a great secret, "So am I," she told him. "And guess what, Pa! Ransom is a minister! He's going to be ministering in Kentucky with his father."

Suddenly, John sobered. He stretched forth his hand to Ransom. Ransom shifted the package in his arms and shook his hand. "Son, I'm glad to hear that Rachel married a good man. I've been awfully worried about her, and to know that she's married to a man of the cloth eases my mind considerably."

Ransom nodded to John. "I'm the fortunate one, sir."

∞∞∞∞∞∞∞∞∞∞∞∞∞∞

At Ransom's suggestion, Elizabeth flew into action and scheduled a surprise birthday party for Rachel at the inn. She wanted to make it a grand gala, but Jacob suggested that since the town was getting packed and ready to leave for Kentucky, it was probably best to keep it a small affair. She found, to her dismay, in her planning, that the guest list grew larger by the hour. "Oh!" she thought to herself. "I couldn't possibly leave out Gerald and Martha Miller! And Doctor and Lydia Stone and the Dicksons and the Carsons. Oh! And of course...."

Ransom and his parents left early for the inn under the pretense that John and Rachel might like to spend some time alone.

Rachel studied her father as he chatted about the road they would be traveling and the land that was their destination. Streaks of gray tinged his black hair and lines were deeply etched into the contours of his face, carved by the outdoors. Gone was the restlessness that had caused him to leave her behind, and in its place, there was now a peace she had never known him to possess, even when her mother was alive. She supposed his relationship with God had brought about this miraculous change...a welcome change at that.

Rachel had missed him so this last year and she instinctively knew he did not realize how much his leaving her behind had devastated her. His adventures in Kentucky were rugged, she was sure of that. But she would have endured anything just to be with him. Growing up, she was his shadow, his pride, loving the outdoors as he did, hunting, fishing, and working the land alongside him, shoulder to shoulder. Then he'd left her with the Templeton family, uprooting her from the farm that was her life, without so much as goodbye or a backward glance.

How often she had cried out for him, for the comfort only he could give, and how bitter the knowledge he might not come back for her!

In spite of their reunion, the unspoken chasm created by his departure, still lay between them and she was tempted to talk about her mother to bridge the gap. Looking at his worn face, "Better to leave it for another time," she thought. So much had occurred during his absence, and the events of the past year ran randomly through her mind as her father rambled on.

"What was that, Pa?" she asked, as her mind came back to the present.

"It's nearly seven o'clock, Rachel." Sitting on the settee, John Winslow stretched out his long legs. "What say we take a stroll up town and see what's going on at the inn?"

"Sure, Pa." Rising, she said, "Let me change first."

As she was upstairs, John looked around at the room. Beautiful ornate furniture, carved meticulously, it was the finest he had ever seen. Rugs of brown and yellow hues lay on the floor, inviting guests into a plush lifestyle he had never known. He was raised a Quaker, and their philosophy had been plain and simple.

The best of everything. Yes, it was a good thing that he'd brought Rachel to this household. She had known only the cloistered, crude surroundings of a country cabin at the farm. It was best that she saw how some others lived.

As she came down the stairs, dressed in a white muslin frock, the breath caught in John's throat, as he saw the exact image of Rachel's mother. His mind raced back to what he had tried so hard to forget in his wanderings the past year. Emily—a gracious lady—the heartbeat of his life, and the sickness that had taken her from him so quickly.

He noticed every detail about Rachel for the first time since returning. How her dark eyes danced, how small her hands and waist were!

He moved to the foot of the stairs and leaned on the banister. "Rachel!" he said, as gently as the constriction of his throat would permit, "You look just like your mother."

Rachel smiled and took the arm he offered. As they left the parsonage, he covered her hand with his and said laughingly, "You know, you were kind of wild as a child. I know it was my fault. I guess I treated you like a man would his son." He turned toward her, "Rachel, if your mother could only see you now, she would be proud what you've grown into. You've even matured into her graceful ways."

Rachel didn't feel so graceful. Oh, she was indebted to Elizabeth and her sisters-in-law for teaching her the essentials of societal etiquette. Not that she always fulfilled them, nor wanted to. At least, now, she didn't always feel that she made a *complete* fool of herself.

Sighing inwardly, she closed her eyes and remembered the scent of fields sprinkled with colorful wildflowers. She frowned and opened her eyes. She detested city life.

Something John was saying brought her back to the moment. "What did you say, Pa?"

"I said—marriage has certainly agreed with you. I'm glad you found a good man."

A frown furrowed her brow, as she thought, "Is this the right time to tell him all I've been through? What would he think of me if he knew that I'm divorced?" Finally, she reconciled herself to the fact that honesty, rather than deception, would be right at this point.

"Pa, there are some things I need to tell you," she said, determination in her voice. "I don't want you to get upset, but I think you need to know."

As they strolled along toward the inn, she revealed her last year filled with sorrow and hardship. There was a moment of silence as they reached the inn. Rachel feared her father's reaction was disgust at the foolish decisions she had made. John stopped, and turned her toward him.

Remorse filled his voice. "Rachel, girl, I'm sorry. I should have been there for you. I had no idea." He put his finger under her chin, tipping her face up towards him and asked, "Can you ever forgive me?"

She smiled at him, as she realized the chasm had been crossed. "Oh, Pa…I forgave you a long time ago. You know I've always loved you. Besides, the Lord moves in mysterious ways. That's what Reverend Templeton says, anyway. I think His will is being worked out in spite of everything that has happened." She hooked her arm through his. "Come on. Let's go inside."

CHAPTER EIGHT

THEY STEPPED THROUGH THE DOOR OF THE INN and her hand flew to her mouth as "Surprise" was shouted out in unison. A small band began to play a waltz and Ransom instantly pulled her onto the floor to dance. Overcome with shock, Rachel looked into his eyes. As she stumbled, he pulled her closer and said, "Just follow me, Rachel."

"How—when did you plan this?" she asked, when she finally found her voice.

"Mother and I whipped it up last night. I take it you're surprised?"

"Surprised? I didn't even think you'd remember that tomorrow is my birthday."

"How could I forget *anything* about you?"

She giggled.

Tom McClelland and his brother Robert were standing with Sam at the buffet table watching them dance. Cordelia walked up with three-year-old son Adam and seven-month-old daughter Starr. Cordelia fixed a plate from the buffet for Adam and turned a chair around to use as a table for him.

She handed the baby to Tom and said, "Here, Tom, watch the children. I'm going to dance with my husband and then I'm going to put the children to bed." She turned to Robert, "We haven't danced since we were married, dear."

"Well, Sam," Tom said as he adjusted the baby in his arms. "It looks like you and I are the only ones without partners tonight. That's pretty unusual, for you always had some good-looking girl flitting around, vying for your attention."

Sam laughed. "Yes, I know. Please, don't remind me. I've had pretty much of a reputation in the past, but that's behind me now. This is a new time and a new life. I've committed my life to God and that's the way I intend to keep it.

Watching Ransom and Rachel dance, Tom commented, "They make a good couple, don't they? I'm just itching to dance."

Sam took the baby from Tom and jerked his head toward Ransom and Rachel. "Go. Cut in. Dance with Rachel."

His eyebrows rose. "You think so?" He grinned and said, "All right. Just watch me." Tom was already swaying to the music as he stepped onto the dance floor. Tapping Ransom on the shoulder, he quipped, "Breaking in, old friend."

Reluctantly, Ransom relinquished his hold on Rachel and she laughed as she moved into Tom's arms.

"Watch your toes, Tom," said Rachel. "I'm not a very good dancer. In fact, the only dance I really know is the waltz, and very poorly at that."

"You'll fly like an eagle with me, birthday girl," and he whirled her in time to the reel the band was playing.

Tom danced with Rachel through the next tune also and when they left the floor, Ransom was waiting at the table with a glass of tea for Rachel.

Rachel stood fanning herself with her hand, sipping her drink as Tom took the baby from Sam.

"All right, Sam," he said. "It's your turn to dance with Rachel."

Sam started to protest, but Tom urged him on. "We won't take no for an answer."

Tom looked at Rachel. "Rachel, Sam's the best dancer around. The ladies practically fought for the opportunity to dance with him."

"Really! The best dancer?" asked Rachel, her curiosity piqued as she looked expectantly at Sam.

Juggling the baby as she started to fuss, and giving Sam a nudge, Tom urged, "Go ahead, Sam. It's her birthday. Give her a treat."

Sam refused to look Rachel's way. In a clipped voice, "I'd rather not," he blurted before he could stop himself. "It's pretty hot and Rachel looks as though she needs a break."

Something in his tone forbade Tom from pressing the issue and Tom shrugged his shoulders.

Rachel was dashed by Sam's answer and her face went paper white. That feeling of rejection she'd come to know so well, reared its ugly head again, and insecurity returned with a vengeance.

She felt herself go cold with humiliation. Clammy perspiration, starting under her armpits, began to trickle down her sides. "Did I make a spectacle of myself while dancing? He acts like he doesn't even like me, but for the life of me, I can't think of anything I've done wrong other than the first time I saw him. That must be it. He thinks I'm unladylike."

The enchantment of the party waned, and Rachel wanted to leave. Determined that Sam would not get the best of her, however, Rachel straightened her spine and pasted on a smile.

Catching the bewildered look on Ransom's face, Rachel remembered that he'd said Sam was straight-talking. Just the thought of exchanging barbs with him made her feel nervous, for she felt he would best her in every way. In spite of the heat, she shivered.

The door opened, and in walked George and Margaret Dickson with their daughter Lacy.

Tom gave a low whistle. "Who is *that*?" Turning in the direction of the Dicksons, Ransom and Sam saw that Lacy was the object of Tom's amorous attention. Slight of figure and blond hair, she was a pretty girl.

"Oh, that's Lacy Dickson," Ransom said casually. "They're making the journey to Kentucky with us."

Tom perked up. "Really! This girl has been in town and you've kept her under wraps, Ransom?"

Ransom laughed. "Well, she's coming out from cover now, Tom," he said, giving Tom a jab in the side. "She's headed this way."

Tom leaned in and whispered to Ransom, "Introduce me to her and say a few good things about me. You know what I mean."

Lacy walked up to Rachel, gave her a hug, and wished her well on her birthday.

She turned to the men. "Lacy," said Ransom, "these are fellow ministers going to Kentucky with us. This is Sam Spencer." Sam bowed to her and she curtsied.

"And this is Tom McClelland, who is not only a minister, but an aspiring attorney as well."

"Hello, Mr. McClelland." Her eyes went to the baby. "What a beautiful baby." Sidling closer, she asked, "Is it a boy or girl?"

Tom grinned. "She's a girl. Her name's Starr."

Lacy took the baby's hand. "Hello, Starr. What an unusual name." Looking at Tom, "You must be very proud to have such a pretty baby," she said.

A flush of red started up Tom's neck and reached his ears. "Uh—this isn't *my* baby. She's my niece."

The music started again and Cordelia and Robert came back to retrieve their children. Taking the baby from his arms, Cordelia glanced at Lacy. "Thanks, Tom, for watching the children." Taking in the situation in a quick look, she urged, "Go on, Tom, and dance with this pretty girl."

Turning even redder, Tom quipped, "Miss Dickson, this brazen woman is my sister-in-law Cordelia." They greeted one another and Tom about to dance a jig right where he stood, calmed himself, and asked, "Well, how about it, Miss Dickson? Want to take her advice?"

He extended his hand and led her to the dance floor, and Robert laughed as Tom whirled her away. "I've never seen Tom get so worked up over a girl before. I thought he was going to lose his sensibilities there for a moment."

"I seem to recall, Robert McClelland," Cordelia said as she poked him in the arm, "that you acted pretty much the same way when we met. Remember?"

He smirked at her affectionately. "You *still* affect me that way," he said softly.

CHAPTER NINE

IN SPITE OF THE PARTY ATMOSPHERE, Will Templeton had only one topic of conversation…the trip to Kentucky. Filled with excitement about their journey, he held sway over the upturned faces around him. A successful businessman, Will electrified the men with his talk about Stone Valley, discussing grand ventures he wanted to undertake there.

With a feeling of exasperation, Jane saw that Will had not even noticed her. She'd taken great pains to look her most fetching this evening in a gown of blue brocade. She could have worn a cotton sack and Will would notice no difference.

"Why doesn't he keep his mouth shut!" thought Jane as she made a mouth of bored impatience. "He's spoiling the whole party with his talk about all his plans!"

Depositing their son Jake in Elizabeth's arms, she made her way over to Will.

When she touched his arm, he started and blinked his eyes at her.

"William, my dear," she said in a clipped voice, "may I remind you this is a party? If these gentlemen wouldn't mind," nodding her head in their direction with a tight-lipped smile, "I'd like to dance at least one dance with my husband."

Slightly embarrassed, he turned to the men and said with a short laugh, "I regret, gentlemen, that I'm wanted elsewhere." As the men shifted their stance and cleared their throats, Jane nodded to them again as Will led her away.

As they danced, Will continued to talk enthusiastically about the plans he intended to reveal to the men the next morning.

"Will, can't you take your mind off of business for one moment and give *me* your attention?"

They had married two years ago and it had been rocky almost from the start. She had resented the time he'd spent at the mill establishing his business, and though often he attempted to cut his time there to reasonable hours, she still had seemed dissatisfied. She could never understand his need to be successful and provide a better than average living for her. They seemed to be going in different directions, and he didn't know what to do about it.

His voice had a silky, almost bored note. "Sorry. What do you want to discuss?"

"Has our marriage disintegrated to the point that I have to prompt you on what to say? What's happened to us?"

"Sorry, again. There's so much going on right now with our move to Kentucky."

"There's *always* a lot going on where you're concerned," she replied sarcastically. "You find plenty to say to other people," she whined, "but not to me."

It was true. She had been drawn to him, his energy and success in business, in fact anything he undertook. He applied that same energy to his courtship. He had thrilled her with his attentive devotion and every detail of their engagement. But once married, his attention was elsewhere and Jane felt she received the leftovers of his time. It didn't take long for resentment to seep in and her constant complaining wore thin at times.

"Jane, let's not argue," he said resignedly. "Just enjoy the party."

"You won't even stay with me, Will," she complained. "You're running around talking to all the men. It's as though I don't even exist."

He sighed. "Okay. I'll stay with you for the rest of the evening."

"If you stay with me, I want you *really* with me. Pay attention to *me*."

Will didn't want a major fight on his hands since they were leaving in a couple of days. He tightened his grip on her back and gritted his teeth. "I promise. I'll pay attention to you for the rest of the evening."

Rachel found herself drawn by Ransom to a dimly lit corner of the room.

"Have I told you today that I love you?" Ransom spoke softly, a smile in his voice.

Laughing, she answered, "Yes. As a matter-of-fact...three times."

"I'm telling you for the fourth time, then. I love you. You've wrapped yourself around my heart. You know that, don't you?"

She gave a little snort. "Oh, Ransom, I haven't purposely done anything of the sort."

"I didn't say you did it on purpose. You could never do anything like that. If I could stuff you in my shirt pocket and carry you everywhere with me, I would.

"Since I can't, my love," he said, pulling a locket from his pocket, "the next best thing I can do is give you something that will always remind you of me."

Turning the locket over, he read the inscription to her, "All my love, always."

"Oh, Ransom!" she exclaimed as she fingered its delicate, filigreed finish, "It's beautiful!" She opened it and asked, "But isn't there usually something inside?"

"That, Rachel, is reserved for a lock of hair from our first child."

She thought of her little girl, but said nothing.

"Turn around and I'll hook it around your neck," he said, as he clicked the locket shut.

She turned and gathered up her hair while he fastened the chain.

Turning her to face him, he held her gaze. "If you ever doubt that anyone loves you, just take the locket and read it. Those words will always remind you of my undying love."

"Ransom, you're so good to me."

"Happy birthday, Rachel."

Looking swiftly at the crowd, he then bent his head and kissed her cheek.

Sam was standing at the buffet, discussing the upcoming trip with John.

In the reflection of the mirror, Sam watched the gift-giving scene play out and his appetite vanished when Ransom bent to kiss Rachel. All his feelings about her that were carefully ordered and restrained since their meeting yesterday, began to unravel. He turned his head away from such an intimate scene.

God, I truly wish them all the happiness they deserve. I really do.

Sam bid John goodnight and headed to his room.

CHAPTER TEN

JOHN WINSLOW CALLED A FINAL MEETING at the inn with the men of the party to discuss their route of travel, and to make sure they understood the provisions they would need as they prepared to leave the next morning.

"As I've told you before, men," John advised, "no wagons will be able to travel the road once we reach the Cumberland Gap of Kentucky. The road is only a path once we leave Virginia, so any of you who are still planning on taking wagons will have to eventually abandon them and their contents. Better to only take packhorses with any supplies you will be taking with you. It's easier to travel on horseback, anyway. We've got some steep, mountainous terrain to cover."

Will looked for an opportunity to divulge his plans for those families who had no land to go to and he had plotted a map for a town. It wasn't enough just to be a minister, he reasoned, God had also blessed him with the ability to make successful business ventures. He and the Templeton family were financially secure, but he realized the importance of networking with those who did not necessarily have the means, yet had abilities that could be utilized.

It was better that all worked together instead of just individually, and a town should be established where people could barter and trade and establish themselves in the occupations they were skilled in. Ventures such as wagon makers, liveries, blacksmith shops, millineries, mills, bakeries, shoemakers, and any other area of expertise, would bring others into the area where ministry could also flourish.

Will raised his hand and motioned for permission to speak. Clearing his throat, "I've decided to deed forty acres of my parcel of land to the families who do not own any land." Unrolling a survey of his land, he pointed to an area on the map. "I've laid out lots for homes and lots on the main street for businesses. My sawmill equipment should be in Stone Valley when we arrive and with all the manpower between us, we should be able to raise homes in very little time. We can establish this as a town where we can build a school and church."

He paused. "I think we're all grateful that Colonel Wellington donated his land grant to the organization." Then glancing at Jacob for approval, he continued, "I've been thinking that since Colonel Wellington was instrumental in establishing this town, and since he is also providing the land grant in Kentucky, it would be good to name the town New Wellington, after him."

The approximately forty men who had gathered there began to murmur. One of the men shouted, "Yes!" in affirmation and the others joined in, enthusiastically voicing their consent.

"New Wellington, it is, then!" shouted Will.

Jacob held up his hands to quiet the men. "The next order of business is to appoint a committee of seven to supervise the public buildings to be built and assign which lots will go to which families. Any volunteers, or shall I appoint?"

"I volunteer!" exclaimed George Dickson.

"Very good, George. Anyone else?"

Egan Carson, Matthew Grantland, and Gerald Miller raised their hands.

"All right. Anyone else? No one? Then I take it upon myself to appoint Sam Spencer, Tom McClelland, and Will Templeton. Congratulations, men."

∞∞∞∞∞∞∞∞∞∞∞∞∞∞∞∞

Before sunrise the next morning, eager travelers began meeting at the livery with their packhorses. The packsaddles were fitted with thongs with which to tie on the bundles. Huge baskets and bundles of clothing, bed furnishings, tents, sacks of seed, farming and household articles were prepared and secured and balanced upon both sides of the horses. Those who had not shipped their goods down the Ohio had pieces of light furniture strapped upon the backs of the animals. Children were crowded on top, or were to ride in front of or behind their mothers and other relatives.

By six o'clock, the sun was already scowling with the promise of another sweltering day as the fifty families were lining up in procession. The men attended the small herds of cattle, making sure the cows had been milked and the milk poured into canteens for the children. A few dogs were also present as a number of families were reluctant to leave their animals behind.

Gabe Roswell's hounds created a fracas in the midst of all the excitement, tussling, yelping, and nipping at each other, whirling under and around the packhorses, unsettling the horses.

"You, there!" John Winslow growled as he rode up. "Get your dogs in order or leave them behind!"

John stationed some men in front of the party to assure that the way would be clear and some men behind to guard the rear. Tom

McClelland and his brother, Robert and family, and their herds were stationed in the rear guard. Tom was pleasantly surprised to learn that the Dickson family was at the back of the line and he looked forward to getting to know Lacy better in the days ahead.

The Templeton family along with Sam Spencer had purchased a large number of cattle. They decided to trade among themselves the duties guarding the front line and driving the herds.

Jane was saying tearful goodbyes to her parents as Will watched from a distance. She was bitter over his decision to leave Wellington. Every argument and plea to him in the last few days did not persuade him, for he felt this was God's direction for their lives.

He knew Jules and Katharine would miss Jane and the baby, but they didn't argue with him. Knew it wouldn't do any good.

"I don't want to leave Wellington," Jane sobbed, wiping the tears with the back of her hand. "I don't want to leave you, Mother...Father, but more than that, Will just doesn't understand what I need from him. I have feelings of my own and want him to value me more than as just a wife and a mother to Jake. He never gives any worth to my opinions, and without you there, I'll feel so alone."

Jules put his arm around her. "Jane, this is up to you. If you want to stay here, we'll take care of you and the baby, but we can't make that decision for you."

Jane nodded as she leaned her head on his shoulder. "I know, Father." She gave a deep sigh. "I really have no choice, except to go." She lifted her head to look pleadingly into his face. "Could you possibly come and visit me? I'm afraid, otherwise, I'll never see you and Mother again."

Jules smiled at her. "Your mother and I have already been discussing that. Who knows? Maybe someday we'll move down there with you…or at least, visit. We'll certainly pray about it. And remember, daughter, for all his faults, Will *is* a successful businessman. He'll provide a good living for you and Jake."

"Yes, I know, Father," she pouted. "But making a good living isn't enough. I want to be loved for who I am, not *what* I am."

John gave the call to head up, signaling time to leave, and Jane took the baby from Katharine and gave her a frantic last hug. "They're ready to leave now, Mother. I love you and will miss you." As Jane turned and walked away, Katharine broke and began to weep, nearly running after her. Jules put his arm around her and led her away.

John tried to quiet those who could hear, mainly those in the front, and Jacob Templeton offered a prayer for their journey. Then, John's voice rang out "Move out!" as he gave the signal for the party to proceed.

Will took the baby as he helped Jane mount her horse and then handed Jake up to her. Nine- month-old Jake would ride in front of her as Will tended to the front guard and took care of their livestock. He knew her heart was breaking and wanted to comfort her, but he knew that any gesture he made, would be rebuffed. As Jane's horse began its departure from Wellington, she twisted around and looked back at all she had known.

Remember Lot's wife was the scripture that leaped to her mind. She shuddered and turned back around.

CHAPTER ELEVEN

THE SUN HAD BEEN SIZZLING ALL MORNING and after the mid-day break for lunch, groaning was heard throughout the camp as horses were mounted again. They had ridden for hours and the women were not used to being in the saddle that long.

In early evening, John signaled for the party to set up camp. He would have liked to continue longer, but he was aware that if he pushed too hard, especially the first day, he might well break the spirits of those he was leading, the women in particular.

Horses were unpacked and as fires were built to prepare the evening meal, small tents were quickly set up. The men hobbled the horses by tying their front legs loosely with pieces of rope to keep them from running off as they grazed throughout the night. Bells fixed on a leather strap had been hung on the horses and cattle to make it easy to find them in the morning. A straying animal was easier to find with a bell tinkling as it moved.

Jane had been morose the entire day, missing her folks. Her daggered looks had not escaped Will. He handed Jake to his mother to watch and asked Jane to take a stroll out of earshot of the others. They stepped into a grove of oaks.

"You've got to snap out of this, Jane," he informed her in an exasperated tone.

"That's easy for you to say," she accused as she wiped the tears from her face. "You've got your family around you and I've had to leave mine behind."

Will blew out his breath noisily. "I understand that you're missing your folks. But you've got to realize that many of the families with us have left their folks, also. If you continue on like this, you will infect the other women with your attitude and we'll have chaos on our hands."

She gave her head a toss. "What do you suggest I do?" she demanded. "Quit missing my family?"

"No," he said, "I'm not saying that."

He placed his hands on her shoulders. "It's only natural that you're going to miss your parents, but you're a minister's wife and it's your responsibility to encourage the other women."

"Will, I don't know if I'm cut out to be a minister's wife—not in this kind of situation," she said crisply. "When I married you, I expected to spend my life in Wellington, in our church, and with my family."

Will withdrew his hands and stared at her. Though he was a successful businessman in Wellington, as a minister he understood the commitment of following God's call wherever it led, whatever the cost might be. Even leaving his established businesses.

As he looked at her drawn mouth, he realized that she had no concept of the requirements of ministry, or if she did, she didn't care. She was spoiled, he knew that when he married her, and he began to doubt the decision he made by doing so.

When he finally spoke, he chose his words carefully. "You may not be cut out to be a minister's wife, but nonetheless, I *am* a minister.

"Let's settle this here and now, Jane. I am committed to following the leading of God, which at this time, is to Kentucky. If you choose not to go…then you should return to Wellington tomorrow. This is our first day out, and should you make your mind up to go back, then I will have someone to escort you. It's your choice. But understand this, if you decide to continue on, it will have to be on my terms."

Jane was shocked and her features stiffened. Will was willing to leave her behind. That, she never expected from him.

Crossing her arms, she narrowed her eyes, "Which are?" she defiantly asked.

"No talk of missing your folks. If you want to do so when we get to Stone Valley, then I will understand. But while we're relocating all these families, it's important to keep morale high. Understand, Jane, the journey will get tough. There's danger ahead, and the people will get tired. It's important for the leadership to keep a face of encouragement, no matter how we feel."

He softened his voice. "We're servants of the people." Putting his hands on her shoulders again, he said, "That's what ministry is about, and you will have to realize that you are an example to the women. Your mind has to be resolute to that fact."

She uncrossed her arms and shook her head. "I don't know, Will. I don't know if I have what it takes to do that. I'm scared. I've never had to turn my back on everything and everyone before, and I feel so alone."

He thought about that for a moment then put his arm around her. "I suppose you're right in some respects. After all, my family is with me. I haven't really taken that into consideration. But I'll try to see things from your point of view. I'll be there to encourage and help you all that I can. Just promise to keep your thoughts to yourself for now."

Smiling at her with his old charm, he asked, "Agreed?"

She looked up at his soft, brown eyes. He could be quite human sometimes. She really did love him and wanted to be what he wanted her to be. She gave a little smile, and in a small voice said, "All right, Will. I'll try."

He walked her back to their campsite. He knew she had settled down temporarily, but he had no illusions about the future and knew there would be stormy days ahead.

"Well, the Bible says married people will have trouble," he thought.

CHAPTER TWELVE

"HOLD STILL," George Dickson hissed at his horse.

The horse resisted having his front legs tied, and tried to nip George as he and Tom tended to their livestock.

The young women were at the water's edge dipping water into wooden buckets to take back to camp. Lacy Dickson was toting her filled bucket back to the camp, intending to bring back another to fill.

Straightening up from his horse, and catching sight of Lacy's blond hair, Tom gave a good-natured slap to the animal's rump.

"Finish up for me, will you, George?" Tom asked.

Without waiting for a reply, "Let me help you with that, Miss Dickson!" Tom shouted as he ran towards her.

Lacy plunked the wooden bucket down on the ground. She smiled as he reached her. He picked up the bucket, and she gushed, "Oh thank you, Mr. McClelland." With an engaging smile, she looked sideways at him. "Men have such an advantage over women...you know...their physical strength."

Tom was startled, and then ecstatic, as he realized she was flirting with him. He'd never been one who could initiate such conversations with women. Most of the girls he knew had considered him a trusted friend or like an older brother and treated him that way. Though he was good-looking enough, with light brown hair and eyes, he'd never been more than a confidant to broken-hearted girls wishing to unload their problems. In fact, when he was in the company of several girls, sometimes they forgot he was there and shared some intimate thoughts told only in a group of females. This had taught him a lot about the workings of the female mind and growing bold, he dared to flirt back.

"Yes, well, we all have a purpose in life, especially when someone can help a girl as pretty as you," he exclaimed, his eyes sparkling with pleasure.

Her eyes lit up, warming to the compliment. "Why, Mr. McClelland! You really think I'm pretty?"

"One of the prettiest girls I've ever seen." He smiled. "Thought so the first time I laid eyes on you at the inn."

"You did?" Lacy asked, wide-eyed.

"Absolutely. I made sure that Ransom introduced you to me. And something else, I was very pleased to learn that your family was traveling in the back of the party with mine."

This is easier than I thought it would be, he thought. Reaching the camp, he picked up the other bucket and started for more water.

"Wait!" Lacy shouted after him. "I'll go with you."

Robert overheard the conversation and smothered a smile as Cordelia exclaimed, "Well, I hope he realizes we need water, too."

"Oh, he does," Robert assured her, "he does. Let little brother alone. He's trying to catch a wife, and it looks like she may be easy to net."

∞∞∞∞∞∞∞∞∞∞∞∞∞∞

By sundown, the whole camp had retired for the night in their tents. Ransom noticed Rachel was not herself this evening. Something was on her mind, but with the family around, he hadn't had her alone to himself.

"Are you all right, Rachel?" he asked as Rachel lay in the semi-darkness beside him.

"Yes."

"Your mind seemed a million miles away tonight. Not missing home, are you?"

"No. Not as long as I'm with you. Besides, there's nothing back there anymore to miss."

Rachel grew silent for a while and Ransom thought she'd dropped off to sleep.

"Ransom?"

"Yes?"

"Is there something wrong with me?" she asked quietly. "I mean, well...I don't know what I mean."

"What are you getting at, Rachel?"

"Well, it's about Sam. I know he's your friend, but he's so cold toward me...it's as if he doesn't like me. I tried to think, but I don't believe I've done anything to offend him."

"I don't know that you've done anything, Rachel, but I doubt if Sam thinks about it one way or another."

"Do you think he knows I'm divorced?"

"It could be," Ransom said quietly. "Sam knows a lot of things."

Ransom shifted his position. "Go to sleep. Everything will be fine."

She wasn't so sure about that. Something about Sam Spencer bothered her. From his refusal to dance with her at her birthday party and his snubbing her on the trail, it was obvious he didn't like her. And the fact that his camp was next to theirs, didn't make things any easier.

CHAPTER THIRTEEN

IMPATIENT TO RESUME THEIR JOURNEY, John Winslow woke the party as he rode down the line, stirring everyone from sleep. He had been up long before dawn, scouring the area and checking on the horses and other livestock.

A sliver of the sun's morning rays penetrated the darkness of the camp, and at John's urgings, the party roused from their tents, prepared, and ate a hasty breakfast. The women packed their belongings, preparing them to be hoisted into the baskets on the packhorses. The men unhobbled the horses and rounded up the grazing cattle, wrapping cloth on the clappers of the bells to silence them, and seeing that the milking was done quickly, as John's constant prodding sped up their departure.

Sam Spencer, James Templeton, and Gabe Roswell had left camp early with their packhorses to hunt game for the party.

John and the party agreed to meet up with them at the Anderson Blockhouse, if not before, where they would start traveling on the Wilderness Road. Most likely, other hopeful migrants from Virginia, Tennessee, or North Carolina would be waiting there to join their party in their trek to Kentucky, John informed them.

∞∞∞∞∞∞∞∞∞∞∞∞∞∞

Crack! The report of a rifle rang out. Crack again! Someone had spotted game. Another crack! As Sam decided to move cautiously and find James and Gabe, a doe ran through the grove of white oaks he was standing in. Swinging his rifle to his shoulder, he pulled back the hammer from half-cock to full cock and fired. The doe fell to its knees then slowly slumped over on its side. One deeply drawn breath and it was dead.

Hearing Gabe's barking dogs and stepping into the clearing, he spotted James and Gabe kneeling by their quarry. Gabe slit open the stomach of each doe they had killed and searched until he found a honeycombed-shaped mad stone.

"Aha!" Gabe declared triumphantly, rising and holding the trophy in a bloodied hand. "We can use this for rabid bites. Great for drawing out the poison. Guess we ought to give it to Doc Stone for safe-keeping."

The three men loaded the deer on the packhorses. The sky became overcast as ominous clouds quickly rolled in, and the trees rustled as gusts of wind blew.

Leaning against a horse and peering at the clouds, James remarked, "Looks like rain moving in soon."

"Maybe we'll get some relief from this heat," Sam answered, tying the last doe on a packhorse.

No sooner were the words out of his mouth, when a flash of lightning streaked the sky, followed by a frightening crash which shook the ground.

"Whoa," Sam calmed the alarmed, snorting horse, stroking his mane.

Looking up, Gabe stared at the putty-colored clouds. Since leaving Wellington with the party, he'd been itching to investigate his old hunting ground around the Holston River. Taking off his floppy hat and scratching his head, he said, "I think I'll ride on ahead. Tell Winslow I'll meet up with him at the blockhouse."

And without another word, he plopped his hat back on, threw his big frame over his horse, and rode south with his yapping dogs following.

"That Roswell sure is a strange one," remarked James. "Reckon where he's headed?"

Sam shrugged his shoulders and mounted his horse. Roswell, indeed, was an odd man. A rough-looking man, it was hard to get more than two sentences out of him.

"Who knows?" Sam commented, looking at the disappearing rider. He jerked on the lead line, and they started for the caravan.

Barely had they left the meadow when the sky opened up, stinging them with pelting raindrops.

∞∞∞∞∞∞∞∞∞∞∞∞∞∞∞∞

In the 1760's, Gabe Roswell, at the young age of thirteen, had been among those commonly known as Long Hunters who hunted over the territory between the Clinch and Holston Rivers and the Cumberland Mountains in what was known then as westernmost Virginia.

Gabe hunted deer only for skins at that time. He would skin with a stroke of the knife up the stomach from the tail to the neck, then circling the top of each leg and around the neck. Snouts and shanks were then trimmed off with precision. His camp-site included a spring that he dammed up to make a deep pool in which to put his skins, where they soaked until he had time to scrape the hair and fat from them.

His rifle was a Pennsylvania rifle, invented by an unknown gunsmith in Pennsylvania, ideal for shooting game or Indians. In the gun, a cloth patch engaged the rifle grooves and protected the shape of the lead ball. A limber hickory rod was all that was needed to force the patch and bullet down onto the powder at the bottom of the barrel. The patch kept the ball from rolling out if the barrel was tilted downward. The Pennsylvania rifle became *the* gun going west with the settlers over the Wilderness Road. He kept that rifle for years.

After his wife and son had been killed by Indians, Gabe had moved to the community of Wellington, settling several miles northeast of it. He had become somewhat of a recluse and decided only one person would ever hear the story of his past, and that person would be Jacob Templeton.

He didn't care much what others thought about him, and was quick to notice the ladies avoided him. Not one to bathe often, he had grown immune to his own smell. He was not a religious man, but neither was he irreligious. His connection with the land and its creatures led him to believe there truly was a God. He also believed if there ever was a Christian, it was the Reverend Templeton.

It had been many years since he had been to the hunting grounds and the thought of returning filled him with a sense of anticipation he had not felt in a long, long time. The peace that eluded him through the years after his family was killed began to seep into his heart and he was looking forward to Kentucky.

As he hastily rode to his old hunting ground, Gabe's mind drifted back to those young years of being a Long Hunter. He recalled the days when game had not been gun-shy, because it had never been exposed to humans. Often, in those days, he would find a runway where deer, being creatures of habit, would travel a beaten path. He would often kill several all at once before they became skittish and avoided the runway.

Focusing on a herd to kill for the skins, he would raise his rifle and position it against his right shoulder. Pulling the hammer back from safety to full cock, he fired, causing the deer to jump and drop dead. The others would stir but continued to graze. Only after he had killed four or five did they flee for safety.

Buffalo had been abundant then, also, but Gabe was a realist. This was 1794 and wildlife would not be as plentiful in that area now as it was then. The Long Hunters would have long ago diminished the supply of game.

Settlement would also have increased, but something was drawing him back to a time when all was right with his world, when his wife and son would always be waiting for him to return. The iciness that had settled over his heart after their deaths began to thaw as he rode along. He would be disappointed about the changes in the old hunting ground, that he was certain.

This was not a hunting excursion for him. He felt the need to search his soul and now after so many years he wanted to move on with his life. Move on past the bitterness that held him captive to the days gone by. He wanted to be able to feel the warmth again of sharing his life with someone he loved. Surely, there was still something worthwhile in life and he intended to find it.

CHAPTER FOURTEEN

THE PARTY HAD STOPPED and was setting up camp when James and Sam rode in. The rain had finally let up and everyone in the company was soaked to the marrow in their bones. Tents were being erected and fires started and women were peeling wet clothes off children.

"Looks like you had good success!" Jacob exclaimed as they dismounted.

"Where's Roswell?" John queried.

"He said to tell you that he'd meet you at the blockhouse," Sam answered.

"Where'd he go?"

Sam was untying the game. "Didn't say," he threw over his shoulder.

John didn't like anyone running off from the party like that. It was hard enough keeping an eye on everyone, which included making at least two trips through the caravan each day.

"No indication at all?"

Sam pulled the deer off the horse and it hit the ground with a thud. "No," he answered, unconcerned.

"Good thing he didn't have livestock to take care of," John remarked.

Sam nodded his head and said, "True."

"And now we've one less man to help with the hunt. At least for a few days."

"Won't we be able to resupply?" Jacob asked.

"Sure," John answered easily. "There're towns along the way until we reach the blockhouse, but resupplying means spending money. Some of these folks don't have much and I'd prefer we resupply by hunting."

"Well, what's done is done," commented Jacob. "We'll make out just fine."

After tending to the livestock, the men gathered together to butcher the deer and laughter could be heard as Sam entertained them with exaggerated accounts of the hunt. The haunches were given to the women to cook as the men cut the rest of the meat into strips and set it on sticks to smoke above smoldering fires to make jerk.

Tom was on guard duty and Lacy made her way to the Templeton camp, and meeting Cissa and Rachel, decided to walk to the creek to bathe and wash their hair. Lacy's main topic of conversation was Tom as she dreamily rehearsed every detail of their brief time together.

After about twenty minutes of hearing about Tom, "I think you're in love with the man, Lacy," Cissa observed dryly as she threw Rachel a glance, looking for a sign that she thought the same thing.

"I think you may be right," Lacy said, smiling in agreement.

"Any plans for marriage yet?" Cissa teased as she bent her head over trying to wring the water from her hair.

Lacy blushed and lowered her head as she stored the precious soap back in its container. "As a matter of fact there are. We're thinking about getting married when we reach the Anderson Blockhouse."

Cissa stilled her hands and angled her head toward Lacy.

"Married?" she asked aghast. Cissa straightened as her wet hair fell on her shoulders. "You've only known each other for a few days. Engagement usually lasts at least a year. Don't you think you'd better take some time and think about this?"

Lacy slammed the container shut, "No," she countered defensively. "We've made up our minds. Mother and Father are agreeable." Lifting her chin, "And why wait a year when we love each other?"

Rachel agreed with Cissa. Then...her own past behavior pricked her conscience. She hadn't known Peter very long before they married. Didn't know he would turn out to be the abuser that he was. She still smarted when she thought of him and all he put her through. That marriage turned out to be the worst mistake of her life. Sometimes she wondered if she could trust her own instincts about anyone since she had been wrong on a number of occasions.

But Tom was different. At least she thought he was. And she felt in her heart that Tom and Lacy would have a good marriage. Tom was Ransom's friend and Ransom knew character when he saw it. Rachel could count on that.

Cissa had spoken out of turn. Taking her comb and carefully combing the tangles out of her long hair, she said, "Well, here in the backwoods, things move pretty quickly," smoothing over the hurt feelings she'd caused and reached over to touch Lacy's arm. With a dimpled smile, she said, "I wish you all the happiness,

Lacy. Really I do. Tom is a good man and I'm sure you'll both have a good life together."

Lacy gave a little sniff and turned the edges of her pouting lips into a slight smile.

"Well, I just want you to know, Cissa, I've never felt this way about a man before. Tom's everything I've ever wanted in a husband. I knew almost right away that I loved him and he loved me," she revealed. "He's bright, educated, on his way to becoming a successful lawyer, and best of all, he's a minister. I've always wanted to be a minister's wife. God knew my heart and sent Tom my way."

As Lacy went on about Tom, Rachel listened to the conversation with interest. She had never felt the way that Lacy was talking about. She had never experienced the unabashed ardor of losing your heart to another. No one had ever tapped those emotions, or any deep vein of passion. Emotions, she wondered, as she listened to Lacy, if she even possessed. Marriage had not awakened those feelings within her. It seemed to her that her present marriage had come about as a necessity. Not that she didn't love Ransom. She did and never regretted marrying him. Apart from her mother, she'd never met anyone as loving and thoughtful as he. But for her, marriage just seemed to happen without any real participation on her part. She'd never spent hours daydreaming about a suitable husband.

Escape was more the word that fit. Escape to or from something. Marriage to escape to the farm. Marriage to escape from Wellington and its criticizing people. Running away was the first instinct she had at any hint of conflict. Peter had divorced her and within a week, she was married to Ransom. She had run away from and into marriage.

Lacy's face shone with happiness. In it was the innocence of a child who had known no sorrow or heartache. Rachel felt much older than Lacy, although, in fact, she was a year younger.

In retrospect, she realized Lacy had not faced the formidable situations she had, and she envied her in a way. Lacy was still unshackled by the cares of life and looking forward to a future filled with promise. She stopped short in her thoughts as her mother's voice came to her as from a distance. "God will not put upon you more than you can bear."

Smiling to herself, she realized she also had a future filled with promise. Perhaps, when she and Ransom reached their land, Ransom's promise to build her a fine home would be fulfilled. A large two-story, he had said, where she would live like a grand lady in their prosperity. Rachel was doubtful about the grand lady part for she still preferred pants to dresses and had secretly stored a couple of pair in their belongings. She preferred to hunt and fish and work outdoors rather than spend time indoors acting like the perfect, congenial hostess with guests. Not that she wasn't hospitable. But she preferred living free and unrestricted. It didn't bother her to be alone for days on end.

Elizabeth and Cissa had taught her the ways of a fine lady, but she felt the lessons imposed upon her were pretentious. Not who she really was. Feeling stifled, she often thought of voicing her objections. However, she knew she'd have to answer to Ransom about that. Ransom, mindful of the opinions of others, often prodded her to be the proper wife, always noting any breach of etiquette, and at times it annoyed her. Still...all in all, she was thankful for Ransom. Good- looking as he was, many of the young women in Wellington had envied her. He had befriended her in so many ways. She was trying her best to be what he wanted her to be.

Rubbing her hair vigorously with her towel, she thought, with a sigh, of how she would love to throw off the restrictions of the life he had known, and his insistence that she live accordingly, and run free in the wind. Sometimes, she wondered what it was about her that he fell in love with. They were different in so many ways. She was raised in almost total seclusion with her father and mother. The land was her familiar friend and nature was her sister. Its smells and sights always lifted her spirits. She was so unconventional, and often without meaning to, caused the ire of others to rise. He, on the other hand, was the perfect gentleman, diplomatic and polite, always knowing the right thing to do and say.

As the conversation between Lacy and Cissa turned to starting a family, her mind was drawn back to the morning when alone in her cabin, Ransom had delivered her stillborn baby.

She'd kept her eyes averted that day and dared not look as Ransom held the tiny, lifeless infant in his hands.

Turning away to hide the tears burning behind her eyes, Rachel pretended to rearrange her comb and soap, clicking the tin container open and shut again. She had never given the baby a name in spite of Ransom's insistence that she should. She would not, could not, for as long as the child didn't have a name, Rachel could stay somewhat detached, as though that little being had never really been a part of her, just some incident that had taken place a few months earlier.

A smile touched the corners of her mouth as she recalled Ransom's conversations about children. His enthusiasm to have a house brimming with them had been the subject of many discussions between them. He hoped signs would develop that she was with child and his disappointment was always evident, when they didn't. He was already planning their future children's lives and looking forward to having his sons educated in the best universities.

Rachel kept her own ideas to herself. She envisioned free-spirited, tough and strong-willed children, able to meet any challenge, fearlessly carving their way in life. Her children would not know her gentle mother, Emily, but they would be blessed to know their grandfather, John. A small laugh escaped her lips as she envisioned John romping with her children, teaching them to hunt and fish.

In her mind, she could see Ransom traveling the district preaching the gospel, winning souls for Christ, and instilling moral values in their children. Yes, life was good and would be even better when they got to Kentucky, for the past would once and for all lay behind them.

CHAPTER FIFTEEN

RANSOM WAS RIDING FRONT DUTY with Frank Morgan when a huge rattlesnake struck at his horse. The horse reared, catching Ransom off guard, throwing him to the ground, and knocking him out cold.

Hearing the rattler and eyeballing it, Frank's reaction was lightning swift. He quickly drew his hatchet and hurled it, striking and killing the snake as Ransom's horse ran off, splashing through the creek and charging up onto the bank.

After making sure the rattler was dead, Frank dismounted and scrambled to where Ransom lay unconscious.

"Ransom!" Frank tried shaking him but there was no response. Surely he wasn't dead! For a few seconds, panic like he had never known set in. Then seeing Ransom's chest heave with a ragged breath, he exclaimed, "Ransom! Thank God!"

He was alive, but Frank couldn't tell if he was hurt or how badly. He took his canteen from his horse, moistened his handkerchief, and wiped Ransom's face, trying to rouse him to consciousness.

The first thing Ransom was aware of when he came to was pain. Pain all over. Pain so bad, it was making him sick to his stomach. Somewhere in the back of his throbbing head came the realization that he was badly hurt. Where was he and how did he get injured? Oh, yes. The last thing he remembered was tumbling to the ground. And something else: the rattle of a snake. It all came back to him now.

"Are you all right, Ransom?" asked Frank, concerned, leaning over him. "Is anything broken?"

Coming fully awake and opening his eyes, Ransom realized one leg was twisted under the other. Blazing pain radiated from his shoulder as he tried to move into position to free his leg.

Gripping his shoulder and gritting his teeth, Ransom uttered, "It's my shoulder, Frank. I think it's busted and my wrist is hurt, too, for it's starting to swell."

Moving as gently as he could, Frank pulled Ransom's leg free, and said, "Don't move anymore. Lie still."

Ransom lay back on the ground, closed his eyes again, and tried to relax, willing the pain to stop. "How's my horse?"

Frank glanced at the horse which had settled by a grove of trees and begun to graze. "He got spooked pretty bad, but he appears to be settling down now."

"I can't believe I was thrown," he lamented. "In all these years of riding, it's never happened before."

"You've been mighty lucky, then," Frank commented. "Guess it was just your time."

Ransom scowled. "I don't believe in luck—or—my time."

"It was just a manner of speech, Ransom," Frank explained.

The thought came to Ransom that he was holding up the party. That wouldn't do. They'd been traveling south a few days and would soon be at the blockhouse.

"Get my horse," said Ransom, "make sure he's not injured, and then go find Doc Stone."

"I'll check on your horse *after* I get Doc Stone," Frank told him. Without giving him a chance to protest, he leaped back into his saddle, and jabbed his boot heels into the horse's flanks, which sent the animal jumping forward.

Passing by the Templetons, "It's Ransom," Frank shouted. "His horse threw him and he's hurt."

Jacob, Elizabeth, and Rachel rode swiftly to the front of the party.

When they found Ransom, they dismounted and started peppering him with questions. Ransom raised his good arm to silence them and then with a grimace grabbed his injured arm again.

"A rattler struck at my horse and the horse threw me. Father, could you check on him to make sure he wasn't bitten?" Turning a smile on Rachel to reassure her, he said, "I'll be fine. Doc will take good care of me."

Elizabeth began to open her mouth to speak again of her doubts about the trip, but thought better of it.

Word of Ransom's accident reached the end of the line and Tom galloped up just as Will rode in from a hunt.

Will was off his horse before it came to a complete stop. Covering the ground quickly and kneeling down on one knee, "What happened, little brother?" he asked, alarmed.

"I got thrown, Will."

Doctor Stone arrived and loosening Ransom's shirt, he probed his shoulder and examined his wrist. Ransom groaned.

"Well, what about it, Doc?" he growled. "Am I going to live?"

"Oh, you'll live all right," Doctor Stone said. "Your shoulder is busted, though, and you've twisted your wrist. And it seems you have a slight concussion, but you'll recover."

"What are you going to do to fix me up?"

"Well," he said, rocking back on his heels, rubbing his chin, "if we were settled, I would bind your shoulder and chest and advise you to remain in bed. But we're not, and the best I can do is to put your arm in a sling and hope it will mend on its own. I can do something about that wrist, though." Turning to Will, he said, "Find me some horse balm and soak the leaves in water. Bring me a piece of tow also."

"Will there be any problems with my arm, Doc?" Ransom asked. "Will it heal all right?"

"Sure," Doctor Stone reassured. "You're young and will heal pretty fast. Just take it easy. Don't exert yourself and let others do the work."

"Great!" Ransom exclaimed with disappointment. "I'm useless and will end up being a burden to everyone."

Doctor Stone scratched his neck. "No point looking at it that way," he said as he searched his medical bag. "There'll be plenty of time ahead for working. It takes a real man to let others help him."

John Winslow, who'd been out doing some scouting, arrived back at the party. Seeing the crowd gathered, he pushed through and demanded, "What's going on? What happened here?"

For the fourth time, Ransom explained his mishap.

"What about the horse?" John asked. "Was he bit?"

Jacob stepped up. "No, thank goodness. Frank killed the snake with his hatchet."

"Good," John said. "We can boil the snake and make snake oil for rheumatism." Surveying the situation, he decided, "Better stop here and make camp for the night, I suppose."

It didn't take long for Will to find the plant. It was a tall, square-stemmed plant with yellowish flowers and a minty smell.

He handed the fragrant plant to Doctor Stone, who tied the leaves around Ransom's wrist.

∞∞∞∞∞∞∞∞∞∞∞∞∞∞

The horses had been hobbled and clappers opened on the cattle and Doctor and Mrs. Stone took supper with the Templeton family that evening. James sat down on the ground beside the doctor.

"I was wondering, Doctor Stone. I often see you gathering plants and roots and such. Can you tell me how you came to know what they are used for?"

"Well, James, there's something called the Doctrine of Signatures. That doctrine holds that God left a mark, a signature if you will, on every plant to show the use for which He created it. For example, heart-shaped leaves cure heart trouble. Hepatica, with its spotted leaves, helps cure liver problems." He fixed a keen eye on James. "Have you an interest in medicine, James?"

"I've never had much opportunity to explore it, but I thought it might be something I'd like to look into someday. I'll have my farm to tend and ministry with Father, but still…." his voice trailed off.

Doctor Stone slapped James on the knee. "When you think you're ready, just look me up. You can study under me."

"Thanks." Giving the doctor a grateful smile, "I just might do that," James said.

The doctor lumbered stiffly to his feet. "Now if you don't mind, I think Mrs. Stone and I will turn in for the night." After checking once more on Ransom, they left for their camp.

James rose and joined Cissa at their tent.

"What were you talking to Doctor Stone about?"

"Medicine," he told her.

"Medicine?" she asked, surprised.

"Yes," he answered thoughtfully. "I've been thinking for some time that I'd like to study medicine with Doctor Stone."

"You never mentioned this to me before."

"It's just something I've been thinking about." He flashed a quick smile. "I don't know how I'll manage, though. I'll be pretty busy."

"Why don't you do what Ransom and Will are doing? Hire someone to help with everything and give them part of the profits.

"Yes, I believe I just might do that. Actually, I've been thinking about it since we left Wellington."

Cissa, suddenly shy, touched his arm. "James?"

"Hmm?"

"I'd kind of like to talk to the doctor myself."

Her answer pulled him away from his thoughts and he turned to look at her. "Whatever for?"

She paused. "I think you're going to be a father."

It didn't sink in right away. Father? He drew his eyebrows together. Father!

He asked, "When?"

"In about six months. About February. You don't mind, do you?"

He threw back his head and laughed.

"Mind? Just wait 'til the family hears about this!"

She clutched his arm and whispered, "No, wait. I don't anyone to know just yet. I want this to be our little secret. Just for a little while."

He beamed at her. "All right, I'll wait. But don't make me wait too long."

Cissa smiled. He would make a great father. So kind and gentle, he was just like Jacob. Yes, she was glad she had married him, she thought, as she settled into the crook of his arm.

∞∞∞∞∞∞∞∞∞∞∞∞∞∞∞∞

Lying in his tent, Ransom was occupied with thoughts of the future. Until today, he had taken the dangers of the journey for granted, but today's accident made him realize that he needed to make provision for Rachel. What would happen to her if he was gone? Who would take care of her? She had her father, but more than likely, he would be gone much of the time serving as guide to other parties coming to Kentucky and driving herds to Virginia to sell. According to law, her money from the sale of the farm had become his by marriage. He now, for the first time, contemplated making a will.

The blockhouse was a few days ahead. He'd ask Sam to draw it up when they reached there. Ransom had the feeling Sam wouldn't like what he had in mind.

CHAPTER SIXTEEN

THE BLOCKHOUSE loomed in view. It was a log building of two floors with the upper story extending a few feet out over the lower one, and port-holes both above and below. The over-jut prevented Indians from climbing up, and provided a position from which the defenders could shoot down on them. The trees and brush had been cleared away from the structure, which had been erected in 1777 by Captain John Anderson. From the second floor, settlers could look out in all directions, watching for warring Indians.

As the party approached, the gate swung open and a small, thin man came out. John stepped down from his horse. "John Winslow," the little man said as he stuck his hand out to John. "I figured you'd be coming through about this time."

"Captain Anderson," John said, as he clasped the captain's hand. "You figured about right."

"Looks like a big party you've got with you."

"About two hundred, more or less."

"Keep your eyes open," he advised.

"I will. We…."

John didn't finish the sentence as Jacob walked up.

"Captain John Anderson—this is Jacob Templeton."

Shaking hands, Jacob related the excitement the group felt about the journey.

Captain Anderson took their fervor in stride. He had seen some go and then come back again when the hardships of the wilderness proved to be more than they had bargained for. He wondered how long it'd be before the thrill would wear off this group of city-dwellers. Not that he wanted them to give up. But it took hardy people to tame the Kentucky land.

"You'll be settin' your sights on Cumberland Gap, of course," he replied, a dubious frown creasing his forehead. "Before that, you have to reach a place called Moccasin Gap about six miles from here," the captain gestured toward the west. "That's the gateway to Indian country, if you don't know," he said, trying to gauge Jacob's response.

The only reaction Jacob gave was to flick his eyes in that direction and then look back at Captain John. "Yes, I know."

John Winslow sensed the captain's doubt about the party's resolve. He'd never cared much in the past what others thought, and why he felt it was important that the captain think the best of these people, John couldn't explain. Except that he had utter confidence in the pastor and his assignment.

The captain took a long, slow draw of his corncob pipe and loosened his stance.

"A man and his daughter from South Carolina been waitin' for a party to come through and join up with." Looking inquisitively at Jacob, he asked, "You headed for Boonesborough?"

"No," Jacob answered. "We're headed for Green River Country."

After a moment's thought, the captain said, "They said their plans were for Boonesborough."

"That may be," Jacob told him, shaking his head, "but I'm a minister and most of these people are members of my congregation. We've received a grant of land and intend to settle a community in that area."

Captain Anderson raked his nail across his jaw, shrugged his scrawny shoulders, and said, "Perhaps these folks might want to join up with you anyway. The daughter is a schoolteacher and the father some big businessman, to hear him tell it."

"Wonderful! We need a teacher," Jacob cheered, disregarding Captain Anderson's obvious slur about the businessman. "That solves at least one of our problems."

The party camped around the blockhouse fort. The men took shifts to guard the livestock and keep watch for Indians.

A fire was going in the Templeton camp and Elizabeth was preparing the evening meal. Reaching to pick up the three-legged skillet, a hand reached out to stop her and she heard, "Allow me."

Rising up slightly to get a look at the person with the unfamiliar accent, she saw a tall woman in her early thirties, with curly red hair.

Intrigued, Elizabeth drew to her full height and nodded to the skillet. It was one thing for a man to make such a request, quite another for an unfamiliar lady.

Setting the skillet over the fire, "How do you do, ma'am?" the woman said, beaming a smile. "I'm Abigail Newgate."

Miss Newgate may have forgotten her manners on proper introductions, Elizabeth determined, but she had to give her high marks for her pleasing personality.

"Very pleased to meet you, Miss Newgate. My name's Elizabeth Templeton. My husband is Jacob Templeton, the minister. Are you joining our party?"

"Yes, I believe so. My father is making arrangements with your husband at this very moment." Entwining her fingers, she continued. "So...you're setting up a community in Green River Country?"

"Yes, we are. A place called Stone Valley. Perhaps you've heard of it?"

Abigail shook her head. "No. We had intended to travel to Boonesborough, but Papa's not too keen about traveling alone."

Elizabeth eyed Miss Newgate's ring finger and noticed it was bare.

"Father was part owner in some businesses in our city of Charleston," Abigail continued.

"Oh? Charleston?" That accounted for her flat, slow drawl.

"Yes. My father is from a prominent English family that settled there. They were into shipping."

"I see."

Never letting her curiosity go unsatisfied for long if she could help it, Elizabeth asked Abigail point-blank, "You're not married, then?" softening her question with a smile.

Abigail shifted nervously under Elizabeth's scrutiny. Not that she was unaccustomed to folks prying into her affairs, especially considering her father's past, but marriage was a touchy topic with her. At thirty-two years of age, she had for quite some time been considered an old maid and the ladies and gentlemen of Charleston, though never speaking of the matter to her face, pitied her nonetheless. And that sat ill with her. After all, anyone who was anyone got married. She was the wrong somebody, at least in their eyes.

Glancing at her, Abigail had to smile too, but it was a dry, uncomfortable smile. "Not as of yet, ma'am. No," she said with finality.

"Never?" Elizabeth persisted.

Abigail grew annoyed, but her irritation quickly faded when she saw the hopeful expression on Elizabeth's face. If Elizabeth wasn't a marriage broker, she could see she came pretty close to being one.

Abigail offered up a confident smile, pushing back the memory of the many slights she had endured from the elite Charlestonians.

"I still hope," she answered honestly.

"Hmm…." Elizabeth's eyes raked over Abigail's tall frame. Impressed with her immaculate appearance, her fresh, clean clothes, and the fashionably tended hair, Elizabeth commented, "I assume from your appearance, you're very educated. Do you have instruction in any particular area?"

"Well," Abigail brightened, "as a matter-of-fact, I was a teacher in South Carolina."

Turning her full smile on Elizabeth, "Perhaps the community could use my services."

"That's quite unusual that you should be a teacher, for it's usually men who occupy such a position." Elizabeth mused, pursing her lips. "You must have had some very good training."

"Oh, yes!" she readily admitted. "Father was insistent that I have the best education available. He hired tutors for many years so that I might become proficient in all areas of basic education." Coloring slightly, she added, "Of course, with his prominence in society and my instruction, the city felt that I was an excellent choice to teach."

Her mind still on Abigail's matrimonial plight, Elizabeth asked, "I'm sure you are a very capable teacher, but have you given much thought to marriage?"

"Well—of course," said Abigail, startled. She'd assumed that topic of conversation was finished. She shrugged her shoulders as a frown passed over her face. She wasn't used to being interrogated like this, especially not by strangers. Abigail started to say, "It just never happened" but thought better of it. It was none of Elizabeth's business. No. Better to keep the past where it belonged...in the past.

Elizabeth's mind began to whirl, wondering who among the party would be a good match. Sam was educated and his flame-red hair would compliment Abigail's own red tresses. No. That wouldn't do. Sam was too young. Not by much...but still—. Tapping her finger against her cheek, she realized about all of the eligible men Abigail's age in the party were taken, except for Gabe Roswell and John Winslow.

Gabe Roswell was a large man, who wore a floppy hat over his long hair. His unwashed salt and pepper beard was nearly as long as his uncombed and unlaundered mane. He was the frequent subject of female chitchat up and down the line as most of the ladies in the party thought he was quite uncouth, unkempt, and ill-mannered. He showed no respect for man or woman and was above all, the ladies thought, a danger to their own gender. He was always working a chew of tobacco, his beard stained with the juice, and one never knew where or when he would spit an arc of amber. The women wished for something substantial between their skirts and the yellowish-brown stream and whispered that one of his saddlebags carried nothing but twists of tobacco.

He could let out a horrible string of oaths and was known even by rough comrades as the best cusser around. He delighted, at times, in the dismay created by his outbursts of unsavory expletives. It didn't matter whose company he was in…saint or sinner. The only time he held his tongue was in the company of Reverend and Mrs. Templeton.

Elizabeth Templeton felt sorry for him. When she looked at him she was reminded of Elijah the Tishbite of the Old Testament who wore hairy garments and a leather girdle, living on locusts and wild honey. She'd heard something in Wellington about Gabe. The story was he had lost his wife and son to an Indian attack. *Likely as not*, she surmised, *that didn't account entirely for his attire or manners.*

She almost chuckled to herself. Wouldn't that be something! The prim and proper Abigail Newgate and rough and rugged Gabe Roswell! No. No. That wouldn't do at all. "The best possible choice would be John Winslow," Elizabeth thought, staring at Abigail's tall frame. "Yes, of course, a good match. Though," she reflected, "John is a mite older than she."

"Well, don't be discouraged," Elizabeth said as she absently patted Abigail's arm. "Surely, God has someone picked out just for you."

∞∞∞∞∞∞∞∞∞∞∞∞∞∞∞

Charleston, first called Charles Town, was settled in April, 1670, with the first 147 colonists arriving on three ships under the leadership of Captain Joseph West. Included among the provisions brought to the new settlement were four thousand gallons of beer and thirty gallons of brandy. The waters about town were so brackish it was scarcely drinkable unless mixed with liquor. In a matter of a few months, Captain West complained that many of the settlers were so addicted to rum that they did little else but drink.

Many of the settlers were indentured servants to a landowner who paid for their passage to America and at the end of the contract, which lasted usually three to five years, would be freed and given several acres of land. Many of the female indentured servants discovered that if they slept with their master, the length of their contract was reduced. Once free, these female servants found the quickest way to a viable income was through prostitution. Thus, debauchery found a strong-hold early in Charles Town, in rum houses where the wenching trade was practiced.

By the time the town's name was changed from Charles Town to Charleston in 1783, Cabot Newgate was firmly entrenched in the unsavory, yet profitable businesses of tippling shops and wenching houses. Wenching was at the top of the list of the vices of Charleston's elite, along with card playing and gambling. Such things were indulged in with open exuberance, and it was not uncommon for the men to frequent wenching houses where the prostitutes easily outnumbered them.

A striking man, Cabot Newgate had charisma as well as a hair-trigger temper that was easily rankled at the least provocation. He had grown up in a prosperous home, but much to the consternation of his stoic English family, Charleston's glittering illicit enticements worked magic on him as a young man, and he never entirely escaped from their grip. After college, though a well-bred young gentleman, Cabot went on to supply a promiscuous lifestyle to the elite personages of Charleston.

He inherited merchant ships upon his father's death, although he would have been left out in the cold by his father had his older brother not been killed in the Revolutionary War. Having been fortunate enough to inherit such wealth, he immediately sold the ships and entered into sordid business ventures with disreputable peg-legged Jack Murphy. Accused of being impetuous by all who knew him, Cabot Newgate never gave much of a thought to anything beyond his next adventure, much less, the outcome of any of his actions.

Until…his daughter Abigail was born. She was conceived of the red-haired madam Polly Ann Parker, but the notorious madam died shortly after giving birth to Abigail.

Determined to give his daughter a lifestyle befitting the family's rank, Cabot saw to it that Abigail was educated by the best tutors available. However, Charleston's elite refused to admit the illegitimate Abigail into their society, much to her dismay and Cabot's disappointment.

To protect her sense of self-worth, Abigail's association with the privileged was strictly restricted and her education ended up serving the children of the wenches.

After she passed the age when most young ladies were married, he determined it was in Abigail's best interest to leave Charleston. And quickly wrapping up his affairs, they departed for the most plausible place—the largely unsettled land of Kentucky.

CHAPTER SEVENTEEN

THE WHOLE CAMP WAS BUZZING after it was announced that Tom and Lacy were to be married.

The young couple wanted a simple ceremony, considering where it was taking place. But ever the socialite, and despite their protests, Elizabeth determined to make it the most festive occasion she could muster under the circumstances.

"I would have liked to have a proper reception," Elizabeth lamented. Biting her lip, she thought aloud, "We could rustle together some johnnycake and spread them with the captain's honey, I suppose."

Johnnycake had become a staple at mealtime and amidst a chorus of groans, Elizabeth held up her hand to cut off their protests.

"With the little flour that we have, that's absolutely the best we can do. Of course, Lacy, I know your mother Margaret would be glad to help."

Glancing at Lacy's hair, "By the way, do you have any lace to make a proper wedding cap?" asked Elizabeth.

For a second, Lacy looked surprised and then shrugged her shoulders.

Elizabeth slapped her hands on both sides of her cheeks. "Well, it's doubtful anyone would have used their precious cargo space for something as frivolous as that. I'll have to send the men to gather some wildflowers."

Swinging about, she instructed, "Jane, you and Margaret can make a wreath of flowers for her hair. And goodness sakes! Who will be the witnesses?"

Lacy placed her hand on Elizabeth's arm. "That's already taken care of, Mrs. Templeton. We've decided on Tom's brother Robert and John Winslow."

"Calm down, Mother Templeton. It will be fine," assured Jane. "We'll gather together whatever you need and get started on the cakes right away. I'll find Will and tell him to take care of Jake."

"Oh, *I'll* take care of Jake," said Cissa as she reached her arms toward him. "I'm sure that between Rachel, Louise, and me, he'll be just fine."

"Thanks, Cissa." Jane was glad to have something to occupy her mind besides thoughts of Will's neglect. "One thing about it," she thought, "he'll have to change when we reach Stone Valley or I'll—well, I don't know what I will do."

∞∞∞∞∞∞∞∞∞∞∞∞∞∞

Ransom and Sam sat at the edge of the clearing with their rifles by their sides, taking careful note of their surroundings. Though they were in sight of the party, this was a dangerous thing to do as Indians could appear any moment, but privacy was difficult to come by in this crowd.

"Now," Sam said in his most professional voice while he adjusted the paper in his hand. "Suppose you tell me what's the hurry about having your will drawn, Ransom? Not that I think it's a bad idea, but you do seem to be in a great hurry about it."

"I don't know," Ransom said, with a slight shake of his head. "After my accident, I decided that this was something I should have done right after we were married. I know you've a lot on your hands with guard duty, your herds, and hunting...."

"No problem," Sam assured him.

Ransom ran his hand through hair loosened from its queue. "Sam, I love her so much that I can't bear the thought of being without her." After a pause, he raised his head. "Still, I have to know that she'll be taken care of."

Sam nodded in a knowing fashion and replied, "Understood."

"I...." he hesitated.

"Yes? Is there something else on your mind?"

"No, not really." Then: "No, that's not true."

"What then?" asked Sam.

"It's probably not worth mentioning."

"So mention it."

Thinking perhaps he should open up to Sam, Ransom hesitated, for there was the chance that he would be ridiculed.

Ransom tried to reposition himself. When he tried to move his arm, pain lanced his shoulder.

"I had a dream."

Sam tilted his brow in a quizzical frown. "A dream? What kind of dream?"

Ransom gave himself a mental shake. What Sam thought about it was no concern of his. None! "It doesn't matter. Let's get on to the making of the will."

"Well," Sam said thoughtfully, refusing to move on, "sometimes dreams are not about actual circumstances, but merely represent something else. At least that's what I've heard. Personally, I'm not much into that kind of thing."

Ransom grimaced, regretting that he had mentioned his dream. Sam was a realist, preferring to depend on facts. He guessed Sam was that way because of his legal training.

"I know that," Ransom explained. "But I feel like it's more than just representation."

Sam studied Ransom. "Ransom, you're probably all wrong about this. I think you're overreacting," Sam chided. "Doing something based on emotions alone can cloud your judgment."

He looked into Sam's face. "My judgment?"

"Yes. Some people make decisions regarding wills they regret later on, and then end up writing a new one."

"You may be right," he said without conviction, "but in the meantime I want to draw this up."

"Fine," said Sam. "It's always a good thing to be prepared, anyway."

Rearranging his paper, he asked, "All right. Give me some facts about your personal and real property."

"I've got that all worked out in my mind. My property in Kentucky is to transfer to Rachel." Ransom looked pointedly at Sam. "This is where *you* come in."

Sam's brows knitted in puzzlement.

"I have my own money and the settlement from Rachel's farm that was sold. You are to manage that money for her until she is twenty-five. Any major decisions about the running of the property, including all financial decisions, should be made by you. Anything she wants to do differently must be cleared through you."

Immediately, Sam was up in arms and rose quickly to his feet. "Whoa, Ransom! Do you understand what you're asking?"

"Yes, I do." His voice was firm.

Sam said, "I don't mean to throw a disparaging light on your wife, Ransom, but you know how stubborn and hot-headed Rachel can be. She won't stand for this, you know that."

"Yes, I do," he agreed, shaking his head.

"Then why—?" Sam asked, throwing wide his hand.

"She'll have no choice," he interrupted with frankness.

"Do you understand the position this will put *me* in?" Sam asked. "After all, I'll be the heavy hand in all this."

"You can take it," Ransom stated quietly.

Sam sat back down again and demanded, "What if I don't *want* to take it?"

"My friend," Ransom countered, "if you truly are my friend, you have no choice."

Sam stared at Ransom and saw he meant what he was saying. Saw that he'd given a lot of thought to what he was asking. But he didn't want to be shackled to Rachel's business affairs. He had his own plans, even secretly hoped that his father might involve him in the politics of Kentucky, perhaps as a congressman. He saw no reason why another Spencer couldn't occupy the statehouse.

He didn't like this. Not one little bit. Not that he believed for a moment Ransom's dream—whatever it was—would come true. But, on a slim chance that it would, Sam didn't want the responsibility of looking after Rachel's estate. He'd been mixed up with women in the past romantically, but not in this capacity. And now, Ransom wanted to leave this duty to him? Rachel...of all people!

"Why should *I* be involved in all of this?" Sam asked, still a little heated.

"Because," Ransom explained patiently, "Rachel is ignorant about finances. Any slick-talking swindler could easily take her for everything she's got. Peter Brogade already tried that." He sucked air through his teeth. "But more than that, she's unaware of how to manage things. She won't know how to run North Star."

Pointing a finger at him, Ransom candidly told him, "You're smart and knowledgeable. You'll have to do that for her. She'll need someone like you. In my opinion, you're the most likely choice."

"What about her father?" Sam asked. "He can take care of her and watch out for her."

Ransom rubbed his cheek. "John won't be staying put for very long at a time. He'll be leading other groups to Kentucky and you know that we've made an agreement with him to drive our herds back to Virginia to sell. He can't be there when she'll need him. So the way I see it…it's up to you."

"What about your father?"

"He'll be busy on his own land."

"You seem to forget, Ransom that I'm receiving five hundred acres, also."

Ransom shook his head. "I know. But Father will be busy overseeing the ministry in a large area. He's beginning to get older now and I don't think he'll be up to managing Rachel's property along with his. After all, it's got to be a producing estate to sustain her. You're young…twenty-five."

"I plan to practice law, also *and* be in ministry. Remember?" Sam asked, a little sarcastically. Running his own estate would take up enough time, without overseeing North Star, too.

Ransom smiled. "I remember. You won't be too busy at law for a while, though." He leaned forward. "That's another reason. I prefer that Rachel have an attorney looking after her interests."

"What about Tom? He's an attorney. He would fill the bill just fine."

"Not in my opinion," Ransom frowned. "He has a family now and won't have time for Rachel. You're single, and as far as I can see, haven't been keen on taking a wife any time soon."

"What about James?"

Ransom shook his head no.

"Will? Never mind," Sam answered himself with an airy wave of his hand. "He'll be in his heyday with all the enterprises he'll have going on."

Sam picked up a stick and absently struck it against a rock, deep in thought. After a few moments, he tossed the stick away. "I suppose you've got me on the hook," Sam frowned, conceding. "But I must say, Ransom, I'm not too eager about taking on this responsibility…should it ever arise, that is."

"There's something else," Ransom stated. Sam gave him a wary look wondering what in the world else he was asking of him. "It's not about the will."

"The hurts in her life have damaged something in her sense of self. She doesn't realize it, but I see it. Rachel has a tendency to live in denial." He paused in thought. "But somehow with time, patience, and your help as a minister, I believe she can gain it back. No one really knows about Rachel's baby except you. She'll have no one else to talk to about it. She won't even really discuss it with me." Ransom looked toward the party, searching for Rachel.

"Rachel refuses to come to terms with it, almost pretends it never really happened. One day it's going to hit her hard, and I'm counting on you to help her. It's at that point I believe her healing process will begin."

"I'll do everything I can to help her, Ransom," Sam promised at last. "But I still think you're unduly concerned. You'll probably outlive me."

Ransom lifted his shoulders then lowered them again.

"Maybe—maybe…." his voice drifted off.

"The past can only hurt her if she allows it to," Sam put in plain words.

"Exactly! You've got it!" Ransom exclaimed. "I knew you were the right person!"

Ransom was asking him to be Rachel's emotional, as well as, financial counselor? He didn't think he was qualified for the emotional part. Besides, he didn't think she would confide in him anyway.

Surely this is all a figment of Ransom's imagination. Sam gave a sigh. *Well, I suppose there's no harm in agreeing with him. He's not going to die any time soon anyway.*

CHAPTER EIGHTEEN

FRANK, WILL, AND SAM stood with the herds outside the blockhouse as Tom came walking toward them.

"Congratulations, Tom!" offered Sam, with a slap on Tom's back. "You've been looking all this time for a girl to marry and you find her on the road to Kentucky."

"Yeah!" groaned Frank. "And we have to risk our lives tramping around, looking for wildflowers when Indians could scalp us at any moment! Isn't that a hoot?"

Will laughed. "Well, you know how it is, gentlemen. We've got to keep the ladies happy, even at the cost of our necks."

Laughter rippled through them.

"You couldn't wait until we got to Stone Valley?" Sam's question drew snickers from the rest of the men.

The good-natured ribbing from the men fed Tom's ego and embarrassed him at the same time and he turned red.

"Aw, quit it, fellows. We just decided not to wait. What difference does it make anyway? Here or Stone Valley?"

Sam laughed, took off his hat, threw his head back, and placed his hand over his heart. "He's in love, men. You know how it is when a man is in love."

That remark drew belly laughs.

"Gotta run," Sam said, still chuckling. "You'd better look for the flowers yourself." He positioned the hat on his head. "I've got some business to take care of."

As Sam turned on his heel, he stopped and his grin faded for Rachel came walking toward them.

"Tom, I was sent with a message from Elizabeth," said Rachel, and she flashed him a smile. "She said to tell you not to dawdle getting the flowers. She wants them by this evening for the wedding."

Without waiting for an answer, Rachel turned to walk back to the blockhouse.

Sam watched her walk away with mixed feelings. Uncertain whether to stay where he was until Rachel was out of sight, Sam decided, "What difference does it make? If circumstances are so unfortunate as to prove Ransom right, I'll be executor over her estate. We might as well try to be friends."

Gathering courage, Sam called, "Rachel! Wait!"

Rachel stopped and turned, giving him a puzzled look.

Striding quickly toward her, he said, "No point you going back by your—"

"Thank you, but it's just a short walk," she interrupted him brusquely and headed once again toward the blockhouse. He stood rooted to the spot for several seconds, as though she had slapped him in the face.

"This is ridiculous," he thought, placing his hands on his hips. "No woman's ever treated me this way, and I'll be horn-swoggled if I'll let one now," Sam muttered under his breath. Unwilling to let her get the best of him, he hurried to catch up with her.

"I was already going that way," he explained. "There's something I need to take care of."

She was silent as she walked on. She hadn't spoken to him since leaving Wellington and did not wish to now. The air was thick with tension as he searched in his mind for some neutral topic. "Um…. it's great news about Tom and Lacy, isn't it?" he asked.

She didn't answer right away. "Yes…I suppose so."

"Why so reticent?" Sam asked, throwing her a side-long glance. "Usually women are all excited about weddings."

She stopped mid-step, forcing him to swing around to face her. "Reti—?" Rachel asked, and for a moment felt her breath catch as she looked into his cornflower-blue eyes.

"Reticent. You know—aloof—reserved," he explained.

Her face grew hot at her lack of knowledge of the word and she felt every bit the uneducated, country girl she was. Without thinking, she blurted out, "I guess so—especially if it's their first."

"Oh?" Sam remarked, quirking one eyebrow at her.

Rachel could have bitten off her tongue for that slip. She thought she detected a thinly veiled note of mockery. Surely, he must know she was divorced. How he found out she didn't know, but gossip traveled fast.

Suddenly the still, hot air was stifling her and everything within her wanted away from Sam. She was glad they had nearly reached the blockhouse.

"Excuse me," Rachel snapped. "If you don't mind, I'm busy right now." She caught her skirts with her hands and hurried away without a backward glance.

He watched as she disappeared in the crowd. Lifting his hat and scratching his head, "The frost in her voice could have killed the vines in the pumpkin patch," Sam thought as he shuddered in spite of the heat.

CHAPTER NINETEEN

GABE ROSWELL ARRIVED AT THE BLOCKHOUSE that afternoon. Thirsty, he passed by the spring outside the fort. Drawing his horse to the flowing water, he stepped down, crossed the moss-covered rocks, leaned in, cupped his hands, and drank. He allowed his horse and dogs to drink from the pool that accumulated here before making its journey downstream, and then started toward the blockhouse.

Suddenly, a tall red-haired woman, exquisitely dressed, caught his attention, coming to the spring carrying a bucket across her arm. A long time ago, in another life, he remembered another woman who had such poise. But that had been a long time ago in Virginia.

However, it wasn't so much how she was dressed, or the fact that she looked out-of-place carrying a lace-edged parasol, that initially caught his interest, but it was because no one accompanied her.

"Beggin' your pardon, miss, but don't you know you shouldn't be out here alone?" He frowned as she reached him. "Indian warring parties are a real danger here."

Looking at him, she thought, *the only real danger is this rough and unkempt-looking man.* The air had been still all morning but a breeze kicked up, assailing her senses with the stench of stale sweat on an unwashed body. He had a long beard and who knew what varmints lodged in the matted hair halfway down his back. It had probably been months since he had seen a bar of soap, much less—laid a hand on one.

He was alerted by the breeze and looked about for danger.

"What Indians?" she questioned, wide-eyed, blinking, and giving a little toss of her head.

"What Indians?" Gabe repeated, astonished, as he gave a returning blink.

With those two little words, he knew no matter how hard he tried to convince her, without an actual Indian raid happening, she wouldn't understand.

"Yes," Abigail said absently, switching the bucket to her other arm and looking toward the spring, anxious to get on with her task. "They said there hasn't been an Indian attack for months."

Crossing his wrists in front of him, "Maybe so," he agreed. "But the fact of the matter is, miss, you never know when they'll strike. Can't take chances, and frankly, it's best you don't come out here alone again. I'll stay with you while you get your water."

"Perhaps he's right. Then again, maybe he's not," she thought. Looking at him askance, she covered the ground toward the spring cautiously as he moved beside her. They were in sight of the party, but this wild-looking man had her a little suspicious. She and her father had encountered some coarse-looking men on their journey from Charleston, but no one as untamed looking as this.

As the water flowed into the bucket, she stole a quick glance at Gabe. He didn't take his eyes off her and was watching every move she made. The bucket full, getting firm footing on the slick stones while juggling her parasol in the other hand, she turned and walked self-consciously towards him. Silently, he reached and took the bucket from her and began for the blockhouse.

Giving him another once-over, "I haven't noticed you among the party before. Are you a new arrival?" she stated nervously.

"Not really," he commented. "I left the county with Reverend Templeton and made a swing by an old hunting ground." He pursed unseen lips under a dense salt and pepper beard. "My name's Roswell. Gabe Roswell."

"Pleased to make your acquaintance, Mr. Roswell," she answered politely, with a slight tinge of primness and a little nod of her head. "I am Abigail Newgate. My father Cabot Newgate and I are traveling to Green River Country with the party. I taught school in South Carolina and as we plan to settle in New Wellington, I have been offered the position of teaching in Stone Valley by Reverend Templeton."

Never one to mince words, he asked, "You're not married, then?"

Taken aback and wondering what in the world his intentions were, she hastily replied, "No." She was quiet for a moment. This was a different time and a different place. She supposed the formalities she was accustomed to in South Carolina were not observed here, and if she was to get along with such backwoods people as himself, decided to relax.

With a little smile that barely touched the corners of her mouth, she asked in her most courteous voice, "And yourself, Mr. Roswell?"

He said simply, "I was married a long time ago, miss. My wife and baby son were killed by Indians."

Abigail was stunned and missing a step, she nearly dropped her parasol. Recovering herself, she deliberated about this strange-looking man. The very thought that this man had been married and had a son, was in itself a shock. Who would have such a man? Immediately, her heart smote her at the prejudiced thought. Seeing the man in a new light, she unconsciously touched his arm, and remarked quietly, "I'm so sorry, Mr. Roswell. That must have been very difficult for you."

Abigail's obvious sincerity disarmed him. A woman's touch was something he hadn't experienced for a very long time. The fact that he was so smelly and dirty made him feel unworthy of her and he instinctively drew back, but her genuineness tapped something within him.

"Don't mention it, miss. It happened a long time ago." Reaching the blockhouse, he handed her the bucket. Tipping his floppy hat, and with a little bow, signaling a little civility of his own, he said, "Glad you could join us. Hope to see more of you, Miss Newgate," and departed with his horse and yapping dogs.

CHAPTER TWENTY

MARGARET, ELIZABETH, AND JANE borrowed the blockhouse fireplace. The heat was oppressive as they dashed around hurriedly, turning out johnnycake for next day's wedding.

The door opened and Gabe Roswell timidly walked into the room.

"Uh…Mrs. Templeton, ma'am? Do you suppose I can have a minute of your time?"

Without turning around, and in spite of the aroma of the cakes frying, Elizabeth's keen sense of smell instantly identified Gabe.

"I'm terribly busy at the moment, Mr. Roswell," she threw over her shoulder. "Could you wait a spell until I can talk to you?"

"Sure, ma'am," Gabe answered as he backed out of the door. "Excuse me, ma'am."

"You know, Jane," began Elizabeth, "I noticed quite a few apple trees here and think it might be a good idea to have fried app—"

She broke off at the scraping of a chair behind her and turned to see Jane clinging to the edge of the trestle table.

Feeling suddenly dizzy, a wave of nausea overtook Jane, and she sat down quickly.

Smoothing her apron with meal-covered hands, Elizabeth asked, "Are you all right, Jane?"

Jane fanned her face with her hand. "I think so. I got dizzy all of a sudden."

Elizabeth walked over to her. "Look at me, Jane." Jane looked up at Elizabeth's face. "Uh-huh. I thought so. How long before your baby is due?"

Jane blinked her eyes. Baby? She thought for a moment then began to count on her fingers. She drew a deep breath and put her hand over her mouth.

"You're right." Her hand slid to her stomach. "Why, I must be almost three months gone by now. I've been so upset about leaving Wellington that I hadn't noticed."

A baby! And at a time like this, when they were uprooted from all she knew. At this moment she resented Will more than ever. Wellington was where she belonged, not some trail going to some wilderness country!

"Well...you need to rest," said Elizabeth. "Go get some fresh air and send Cissa to help me. Go on. Scoot."

The door opened and Will walked in carrying the foliage he had gathered. "Mother, this is the best we could do. We found some ivy, oxeye, and pokeberries. Hope you can do something with these."

"The oxeye and ivy I can use. I guess we can find some ribbon, too. But I don't want to take a chance of having the pokeberry juice spoiling Lacy's dress."

Will smiled as he pictured the couple in the midst of the ceremony, inky liquid trickling down the bride's face.

"You can save the pokeberries to use for ink," she added, "if you have a need for it."

"No, *I* don't. But Father may for his sermons. I'll ask him about it."

Elizabeth shot a look Jane's way. "I'm sending Jane outside to get some air. She has some news to tell you."

What now? thought Will.

"Are you sick?" he asked.

"Sick!" she said. "No—yes, I'm more than sick. I'm—"

Oh, she didn't want to tell him like this, but the hot words rushed to her lips and carelessly she flung them at him. "I'm going to have a baby!"

He stared at her for a few seconds and took a quick step towards her. "Another baby?" he asked. "Are you sure?"

At her look he stopped in his tracks. There was real anger in her eyes.

"Just about as sure as I can be."

She was furious all right. A plan had been formulating in her mind. She was giving Will a year to change. If he hadn't changed within that time she intended to go back to Wellington. Now, realizing she was pregnant again, she felt trapped. How could she return on her own with two babies, and furthermore, would Will even let her take them from him without a fight?

She turned away from him, avoiding his touch, and he dropped his hands to his sides.

"Are you all right?" he asked.

"No, she's not all right," Elizabeth cut in. "She's dizzy and needs to get out of this heat. Tell Cissa to come help us."

Will rubbed his neck and gave a short laugh. "I don't know about that, Mother. James told me Cissa's having a baby, too. She's due about February, in fact."

She put her hand on her chest and exclaimed, "Goodness me! Two babies on the way!" She shook her head and waved her hand at him. "Well," she said in an exasperated tone, "send me in Rachel and Louise. Perhaps between the four of us, we can get this done some time today."

∞∞∞∞∞∞∞∞∞∞∞∞∞∞∞

The women were finally done preparing the johnnycake. Elizabeth was left alone as she put the cabin in order. Her hair was damp with sweat and she walked outside hoping to catch a breeze. Gabe Roswell was leaning again the cabin. She pushed some loose hair under her cap and gave Gabe a startled look.

"Mr. Roswell! I'm so sorry. I had totally forgotten about you. We're preparing for a wedding tomorrow. Tom and Lacy are getting married. So much to do, you know."

"Yes, ma'am. I heard Tom was getting hitched."

Sitting tiredly down on a stump, she took the corners of her apron to fan herself and asked, "What is it that you wished to talk to me about, Mr. Roswell?"

Gabe squatted on the ground and took off his hat. His wild, matted hair belied his behavior as he acted uncharacteristically meek.

Bending his index finger and rubbing the joint against his scalp, he remarked, "I know you're a woman of refined manners, Mrs. Templeton." Scratching his nose and keeping his eyes to the ground, he said, "To tell you the truth, there's a lady I'm interested in. She's a fine lady."

Gabe spat a stream of tobacco juice and then rubbed the juice from his beard with the back of his hand. "I know I'm not much to look at." He hesitated. "I was wondering if you could help me, get fixed up, I mean." Casting a shy glance toward her, he admitted, "I'd like to court this woman."

Eyes opening wide in astonishment, Elizabeth stopped fanning herself, her apron suspended in mid-air. Gabe Roswell interested in marriage? This man who looks like Elijah the Tishbite? Intrigued, she asked, "May I ask, if you don't mind, who the lady is you are considering, Mr. Roswell?"

He flushed and grinned embarrassedly, looking like a shy and sheepish boy. "Miss Abigail Newgate."

Stunned, she stared at Gabe in disbelief. Court Abigail, the daughter of a prominent Charleston businessman? Nearly bursting out with laughter, she would have thought him jesting if it were not for the fact that he had turned eyes on her that were dead serious.

Recovering from the shock, she doubted very seriously that Abigail would show any interest in Gabe. Not the prim and proper schoolteacher brought up amidst and mingling with the city's elite.

"Could you help me, ma'am?" His voice held a tinge of begging. "Clean myself up? You know...make myself presentable."

She hesitated as she looked at his clothes that were dirty and foul with sweat. His hair was especially repulsive, matted with months of neglect. His dark beard was peppered with gray, and she suspected had not seen a razor in years. The stench of long-unwashed hair almost took her breath away. "Quite frankly," she thought, "I would as soon clean up a pole-cat as touch this wretched man."

The temptation to laugh out loud again at the very thought of Gabe Roswell and Abigail Newgate as a couple, almost overtook her until she sobered at the look on Gabe's face.

Deep in thought, she lifted the corners of her apron and began to fan herself again. "Well, Mr. Roswell, if you don't mind my saying so, the first thing you'll have to do is shave that beard. And not meaning to offend you, but you will have to take a good, long, hot bath.

"Of course," glancing at his clothes, "we'll have to find you some other clothing and," she brought herself up short as she began to roll her eyes, "something has to be done about your hair."

Running her tongue over her upper teeth, she thought out loud, "I suppose Gerald Miller would agree to trim your hair since he is a barber."

"No!" said Gabe hastily.

At her quick look at him, he said, "Beggin' your pardon, ma'am. I don't mean to offend you, but I'd rather you do it."

Dropping her apron again, she was puzzled by his request. She'd never cut a man's hair in all of her life. Just why would he want *her* to cut his hair when it was obvious Gerald would do a better job?

"Well…whatever his reason is," she thought, as she resumed fanning, "I'll try my best, although I doubt that all the scrubbing he could do will improve his looks any."

But it was worth a try, especially since his heart was so set on Abigail. She hoped he wouldn't get too hurt when she rebuffed him. And this meant her own plans were awry, for she'd wanted to steer John Winslow toward her. "Well," she surmised, "that's between Gabe, Abigail, and the good Lord."

CHAPTER TWENTY-ONE

THE PREPARATIONS FOR THE WEDDING refreshments were complete. An old tub was dragged into the cabin. Under Elizabeth's commandeering, James, William, Gabe, and Frank carried water from the spring until Elizabeth was satisfied she had enough.

"What's this all about, Mother? Who's having the luxury of a tub bath?" James asked as he carried his fourth yoke of water. She refused to answer their questions and shooed everyone away, except for Gabe Roswell.

"Mr. Roswell, do you own any soap?" she inquired and then snapped her mouth shut as she realized that was a ridiculous question.

"No, ma'am, I don't," Gabe answered, standing patiently, waiting for her instruction.

She clucked her tongue. "I thought not." Pinching her mouth, she said, "Go ahead and get stripped out of those clothes, and get in the tub and I'll get some soap." She quickly opened the door and stepped out. Looking back before closing the door, she ordered, "Now, don't dawdle. I'll be back in a few moments."

Rubbing her nose, trying to dispel the odor she'd been breathing, "I don't know if that man will *ever* come clean!" she thought.

The men walked away from the blockhouse. Will laughed. "It looks like old Gabe is going to get a bath. First for him in years, I'd say."

"Wonder what Mother's got to do with this?" asked James. "Seems mighty suspicious to me."

"You'd think it was Gabe getting married instead of Tom," Frank snickered.

Will raised his eyebrows with amusement on his face. "Yeah, and I'd say there's a woman at the bottom of all this."

"A woman?" Frank asked. "What woman would look twice at Gabe Roswell?"

"A desperate one!" Will threw back his head and laughed uproariously.

Gabe stripped off his soiled clothes and stuck a foot in the water. "Yeow!" he exclaimed as he quickly drew it back. "I believe that woman means to sear me like beef frying in a skillet!"

He gingerly walked to where buckets held cold water and poured them in the tub, mindful that Elizabeth might come back at any moment. He heard her voice outside the door and knocking over an empty bucket, quickly plopped into the tub, scraping his arm on the edge.

She entered the room carrying a razor, soap, scissors, mirror, towels, and a clean set of clothes, obviously undeterred by a naked man sitting in a tub full of water.

For all her prim and proper ways, Gabe saw that Elizabeth Templeton could be a formidable woman without embarrassment when on a mission and he tried to shield himself from her all-seeing eyes.

"Here's the soap," she said, handing it to him. "I want you to scrub every inch of your body, including your hair."

As Elizabeth scurried about the cabin, checking on the johnnycakes placed under fabric to keep the flies away, Gabe was silent for a while, holding the cake to his nose and remembering the soap his wife had made. It was the same smell. Bayberry. The memories came rushing back and he could not push them aside this time. She, too, had insisted that he take a regular bath and for her sake, he did. His son, had he lived, would now be on the threshold of manhood. Every part of him, almost everything he had ever done, was done because of his family—until they were killed.

Since then, his life had not fitted him for living with people. He had invited no friendships and offered none.

"I've brought you a razor and mirror," said Elizabeth, jarring his mind from its far places. "When you're through bathing, shave! I'll be back in about half an hour to cut your hair."

She started toward the door, stopped, and then called over her shoulder. "By the way, those clothes are from John Winslow. You need to stop by and personally thank him for his generosity."

She turned and opened the door. Looking back at him, she ordered, "Remember, I'll be back shortly!"

The door slammed shut. As he looked at the soap in his hand, Gabe thought, "I'm not afraid of man or beast, but that woman gives me the shakes!"

∞∞∞∞∞∞∞∞∞∞∞∞∞∞∞∞

"Is Gabe your Christian name, Mr. Roswell?" Elizabeth asked, as she clipped away at his hair.

"No, ma'am. It's short for Gabriel. Ma told me I reminded her of an angel when I was born. Since Gabriel will have a remarkable entry by blowing the horn on resurrection day, she said she thought my coming into the world was worthy of such a name."

Elizabeth almost rolled her eyes again. She was having trouble controlling those particular eye movements when it came to Mr. Roswell. "Gabriel, indeed!" she thought. "He doesn't look angelic to me!"

Elizabeth finished cutting his hair and was amazed at the transformation. His dark hair, peppered with gray and curled up, indeed gave him a cherubic look, accentuated by his deep slate gray eyes. She'd suspected he was not as old as he had appeared to be.

"Mr. Roswell! You look downright handsome!" She surveyed him from every angle. "Why have you been hiding your good looks behind that garb and mess of hair all these years?"

His face lit up. "Sure enough, ma'am? Can I see?"

She handed him the mirror and he gazed into it, turning this way and that. "Yep. That's what I used to look like." Pleased that she had worked this miracle on him, he asked, "Thanks, ma'am. What can I do for you? Can I help you in any way? Just ask me and it's yours! Anything at all!"

"You can help me by keeping yourself clean and trim," she ordered. "Remember, Mr. Roswell, every woman wants a man she can respect." She cautiously took the cloth from around his neck, careful not to drop any hair, and gingerly picked up his clothes, pinching them between two fingers.

"Now, if you have no objections, Mr. Roswell, I'll burn your old clothes. Might as well leave the past behind."

∞∞∞∞∞∞∞∞∞∞∞∞∞∞∞∞∞

Some livestock were butchered and spits were preparing the meat for the wedding festivities at noon. The party would be leaving the blockhouse tomorrow to resume their treacherous journey, but today would be a day of relaxation and fun. It was a fine day for a wedding. A cloudy sky gave some relief from the blazing sun and the humidity had lowered a bit.

When the vows were being exchanged, Gabe caught Abigail's eye. She blinked as she read the message any woman could read. He was interested—and in her. She was shocked when she realized the Gabe Roswell of this morning was the same Gabe of yesterday. A caterpillar had morphed into a butterfly.

With a self-conscious giggle at Gabe, she thought, "He may not know much about books and philosophy, but I've got the feeling he won't tiptoe around courtship."

She frowned when she thought about his religious views. None that she could see. She couldn't marry a non-Christian, that was for sure. Either he would change in that area or he could look somewhere else.

Yes, she thought as she lifted her head with a determination. She might converse with him, but that would be as far as it would go. Besides…Papa would not approve.

In early afternoon, once the meal was over, Nathan Hargrave, after some preliminary tuning and whanging, struck the bow to his fiddle and the crowd came alive.

Abigail sat down on a three-legged stool. She wanted to dance. Restlessly, her eyes scoured the crowd of dancers across the fort's enclosed yard, the lack of single men noticeably apparent. Everyone was having a good time, except her. Oh, to have to sit here, a wallflower!

Gabe watched Abigail from where he stood with Sam and grinned, as he read the longing in her face. Handing his rifle to Sam, he started around the circle of dancers.

She saw him making his way in her direction and knew that he was coming for her. Knew it as sure as her name was Abigail Newgate.

Gabe approached her and bowed awkwardly.

"Miss Newgate, would you honor me with this dance?"

He dances?

He smiled and Abigail felt her stomach turn over. Goodness, but he was almost charming looking. Not only that, she loved the way his gray eyes sparkled when he looked at her.

She felt the strong pull of her father's stare. After taking note that her father was watching them, Abigail observed Cabot's warning look that said, "You know what I expect of you."

She ignored it for Cabot never approved of any man who wanted her.

"If it wasn't uncivilized," he'd reprimanded, after one of her outings with a former beau, "I would lock you in your room. I worry about your reputation. Reputations once lost, are not easily regained."

"If anyone would know that," she'd thought, "you would."

She loved her father, but nearly every love interest that she'd known in Charleston, had been discouraged by him. Her mind warned her that her father might do to Gabe as he'd always done, scaring away her beaux. At her age, she had resigned herself to the fact that she would never marry. And now, when she least expected it, it seemed as though she had another prospect. And if she was gauging Gabe right, he would not be put off by her father's heavy-handed ways.

Looking around at the crowd, she thought, "This is Virginia, not Charleston. Papa has no influence here and there isn't much he can do on the road to Kentucky."

Abigail looked at Gabe, knowing, that according to custom, if she denied him, she could dance with no other man. She extended her hand, and smiled guardedly. "Um, yes, Mr. Roswell. I will."

Droopy-eyed Cabot Newgate, portly from too much rich food and too much spirits over the years, did little to win the hearts of the travelling party. Blusterous and full of himself, he constantly elevated himself above those he considered less worthy, including the Reverend Jacob Templeton.

Cabot loved to eat and his large, rotund figure proved it. Endlessly recalling the rich seafood dishes, pastries, tarts, and rice breads of Charleston, he scorned the meager fare on the trip— johnny cakes, jerky, and roasted venison. He spurned the cups of cider, milk, and coffee made from parched acorns offered to him at the festivity. "Imported wine from all over the world, only the best," he told them, "*that's* what I'm used to drinking. Rum punch made from exotic fruits."

Protective as ever, Newgate frowned with displeasure as his only daughter danced the reel with Gabe Roswell. Far as he could tell, Gabe was not suitable marriage material for his educated daughter. His displeasure was even greater when he saw the look on Abigail's face.

When Gabe finally presented a breathless Abigail, flush with happiness, to her father, the message was easy to read in Cabot's eyes. "You aren't good enough."

Seeing the crowd swelling larger, Jacob grabbed Elizabeth's arm. "Come on, my dear. It's been a long time. Let's see if we've still got a step or two."

As the smile spread wide across her face she said, "Jacob! You make me feel young again!"

"Again? We *are* young!" And with that they whirled off in time to the music.

Ransom and Rachel watched from the sidelines.

"Your mother and father are still so much in love with each other after all these years, Ransom."

"I know. They have a good marriage, that's for sure."

Rachel commented, "And you know what's amazing?"

"What's that?"

"They look ten years younger."

Ransom had to admit this journey had revitalized his parents. Who would have thought that Mother, who loved the city with its stores, would do well in such an environment? Father always said she was a strong-minded woman.

Rachel raised her face to him. "Are you able to dance with me, Ransom? I know I'm not very good, but I'll try."

His good hand rose to massage his bad shoulder. "I don't dare with this busted shoulder." His eyes strayed around the crowd, as couples moved in time to the music. "You go ahead, though, and I'll watch."

"No. If you can't," she insisted, "then I'll stay here with you."

There was a commotion in the crowd. Some of the crowd parted and Ransom and Rachel walked over to see what the ruckus was. Sam was dancing, demonstrating the latest reel.

Rachel's face lit up and she clapped her hands. "Oh! He's absolutely wonderful. I wish I could dance like that!"

CHAPTER TWENTY-TWO

HOPE WAS SWELLING THE HEARTS OF THE PARTY at the thought of reaching Kentucky. They had reached the North Fork of the Holston River, but the river was swollen from the unprecedented recent rains.

They had traveled along a well-traveled wagon road so far. The easy-going would end at Moccasin Gap. Much of the way from there was hilly or stony, and often slippery, muddy, or brushy. Steep mountains would also have to be climbed, no easy task.

John declined to inform the party they would have to wade across swift-flowing streams and splash across boggy meadows, but he sensed that that would not deter them. He had seen some return to Virginia while on this road, while the majority of those who forged ahead were determined immigrants, seeking land that was cheap, with abundant game. Many were looking to get rich, as it had been reported in newspapers that this was truly the land of milk and honey.

He kept to himself the knowledge that some of the smaller settlements in Kentucky had been abandoned after their inhabitants became disillusioned with the isolation and hard work. This party was different. It was large, as the most successful parties were. A ready-made community with all of its social interweaving would help keep the settlement intact and motivated.

John brought the party to a halt and decided to camp near the river's edge. He would need time to scout the woods for suitable logs to prepare rafts to float the cargo over.

The next day was the Lord's Day and in response to Jacob's request that the day be spent in rest and church service, John agreed. Besides, he was hopeful this would give the water time to abate somewhat.

After breakfast was over and the herds tended to, folk throughout the party gathered for the service.

Gabe had no thoughts of attending until Abigail and her father passed his camp.

"Mr. Roswell!" Abigail called. "Are you attending service this morning?"

Cabot glanced angrily at his daughter, but held his peace.

Gabe began to stammer and tried to think of a plausible excuse to give her, but decided none would suffice. He wanted to know her better and in spite of her father, if this was what it took, then, go to church he would. "Be right there, miss." Quickly, he added, "Need to wash up first."

Her beckoning smile told him that he had made the right choice. Anything to please her. It had been years since he'd pursued a woman, but he hadn't forgotten how. Anything or anyone he set his sights on, he usually won in time.

Not that he had much use for church. He had attended a few times with his wife, but never became a Christian. She had been a staunch believer and look where it got her.

Dead.

Whereas he....

He didn't like looking back to sorrows of the past. Since that day long ago when his family was killed, he attacked life with a vengeance, not caring much about anything or anyone. Live for the day was his motto. Take what you can get, when you can get it, anyway you can get it. Not that that line of thought extended to everything. He had a deep regard for children, animals, the sick and weak, and Reverend Templeton.

And now…Abigail Newgate.

Numbness had deadened his heart for years, but since his trip to his old hunting grounds, he was thawing, ready to begin a new life. Living life for so long on his own terms had deepened some furrows within him.

"Can I change?" he asked himself time and time again. "Would I be able to live in marriage again?" he grumbled aloud to himself. There were some adjustments that had to be made if he wanted to find happiness in life again and thinking about it made him nervous.

Never one to be daunted for long, he rallied. "Well," he thought, "that's just the way it is. I can do anything I set my mind to. I'll just have to set my mind a little harder on this."

It never occurred to him that Abigail Newgate might turn him down.

Service had started when Gabe arrived. Abigail and her father were standing at the edge of the crowd lifting their voices in song.

> *Depth of mercy! Can there be, Mercy still reserved*
> *for me? Can my God His wrath forbear, and the*
> *chief of sinners spare?*
> *I have long withstood His grace; Long provoked*
> *Him to His face; Would not hear His gracious calls;*
> *Grieved Him by a thousand falls.*

Reverend Templeton took his Bible and began his sermon.

"My subject this morning is a familiar one," Jacob said, resting his eyes momentarily on Gabe. "Love one another and pray for your enemies."

Not much obvious response, Jacob noted, except for Roswell's narrowed eyes.

"My friends, we knew when starting on this journey, it would not be an easy one. We've been blessed to have good travelling weather in the week and a half that we've been on the road. However, rougher times are ahead. Some of us may suffer loss in different ways, but God has promised to go with us always.

"Jesus said," he went on, "that it is easy to love those who love you, but we must love those who persecute and despitefully use us. Only by God's grace can we do this, not anything within our own selves."

Incensed, Gabe thought, "Is he saying I have to love those low-down, dirty Indians that killed my family?" The temptation to turn on his heel and leave was great and he almost spat on the ground, but something held him there. It was not Miss Abigail, for his thoughts were not on her. Something greater began to churn his insides as the Reverend talked on.

Suddenly, like a light being lit, he recognized what it was. Anger! Anger at a God that would let his wife and son be slaughtered. Anger, because she had served God and He had deserted her in her time of desperate need. Anger, that his future had been ruined. Yes! That's what it was. He was angry! Good and angry at God! He did not understand this God who allowed death and destruction.

His dead wife's face swam before him. Instantly, he knew she would not be pleased with his thoughts. They had been so happy, and his heart began to swell with pain as he remembered. He closed his eyes, trying to shut out the past, but realized the past had been quietly pursuing him and this time would not retreat into the shadows. Instead of the Reverend, it was his dead wife Sylvia who was now saying, "Forgive, forgive."

The Reverend was concluding his sermon. "Sin's penalty had to be paid," he said. "So He sent His sinless Son to be mocked and crucified that we might be made free."

Gabe's head shot up and his eyes searched the Reverend's. "Jesus died for me? He who had done nothing wrong, crucified for me?" His mind was reeling with this information. Sure, he had heard it before in church, but now he *really* heard it.

As the invitational was sung, Gabe felt each word penetrating his heart.

Just as I am without one plea, But that Thy blood was shed for me, And that Thou bidd'st me come to Thee, O Lamb of God, I come! I come!

Just as I am, tho' tossed about, With many a conflict, many a doubt,
Fightings within and fears without, O Lamb of God, I come! I come!

Abigail, without thinking, reached out and touched his arm, expectancy in her eyes. He gave a slight shake of his head as though to say, "Not now. I'm not ready."

Her brows knit together as she moved away from him.

As the crowd dispersed, Jacob walked over to Gabe. Putting a hand on Gabe's shoulder, Jacob said, "God is speaking to your heart, Gabe. See that you turn Him not away."

Gabe nodded and hurried away.

Gabe spent his afternoon with some of the other men preparing rafts for the next day's crossing. Spent physically from the hard work, he heard Abigail call to him as he returned to his part of the camp.

"Mr. Roswell, would you care to take supper with us this evening?"

Surprised by her invitation, he caught the smile on her face and replied, "I'd be pleased, but you don't have to do that, Miss Newgate."

"I know I don't *have* to," she insisted, "but I want to." Her smile began to fade. "I promise you, I'm a good cook," she assured him.

"I believe that." He put his hands on his hips. "All right, let me take care of some things and I'll be right there."

"Thought I'd have to give her a hard chase," he thought, grinning to himself as he walked away. "Looks like she's chasing me. Never been pursued by a woman before. Interesting. How does a man act in a situation like this? Should I play hard to get?" Lifting his hat, he scratched his head and smirked. "Naw." Positioning his hat back on his head, he trotted off, murmuring, "Enjoy it, Gabe, old man. Just enjoy it."

CHAPTER TWENTY-THREE

JOHN CALLED A MEETING with the men.

"I've been easy with the going up 'til now. But we're going to have to put in some long days of traveling to get the rest of the way there," he informed them. "Clinch Mountain is ahead of us and the only passageway through Clinch Mountain is Moccasin Gap. And crossing Moccasin Gap brings us into rough terrain."

Sliding his finger over a map, he said, "Once we reach and go through Cumberland Gap and cross over into Kentucky, we'll leave this road and we don't want our provisions to run dangerously low. The good news is there are some stations along the way where we can restock."

"My family has some to spare should the company need them," Jacob offered. "Plenty of cornmeal should provisions run low."

"That's good, Jacob," John said, nodding his head. "It may very well come to that. I know the road ahead and some days will be slower going than others. Inform the women-folk that we'll be traveling each day until dark. Have them walk as much as they can. The cattle will start going dry with all the walking and not much foraging, so be prepared that your children will eventually have little milk to drink."

"We were thinking it best if a few of us left the party in search of game after we go through Moccasin Gap," Will offered. "Got plenty of bacon and ham for the present, but there's no sense letting our supplies dwindle."

"That sounds like a good idea, Will. Who's going?"

"Well, we're looking for volunteers. Father has volunteered, but he's the spiritual leader here and I think it best that he stay with the people."

Gabe Roswell spoke up. "I'll go." He spat on the ground.

"Sounds good to me," Sam nodded. "I'll go."

James said. "Count me in."

"What about your dogs?" Sam questioned Gabe in a prickly voice. "Leaving them behind?"

"Takin' 'em with me," Gabe answered and spat again.

Sam frowned. He didn't like the idea of dogs along on a hunting trip. The last time they went hunting, they proved somewhat of a problem. They could be useful for scaring up fowl or chasing small game, but they often barked at the wrong time, chasing skittish deer into the brush, and they were notorious for getting snake-bit.

Will slapped his hands together. "Good! It's settled."

"I assume this is only one of many hunts, John?" one of the men asked.

John nodded in a knowing fashion. "You're right. We need to keep our supply of meat plentiful for we're going to get into some rough country. We can jerk some of the meat. That will help get us through.

"Another thing," he continued, "no Indian attacks have been reported on the road since spring, but you never can tell when they'll start again. I don't want to alarm the ladies, but perhaps you men would speak again to your women-folk about taking necessary precautions when leaving the camp. They should never be alone."

The party crossed the Holston River the next morning without incident, and began traveling up higher into hill country. Many had not seen the likes of the territory they were entering. The trail twisted and turned. The path had been widened in some places, but was barely wide enough to let loaded horses in double procession, pass between the thick trees traveling up toward Moccasin Gap.

When the party stopped to rest, Rachel sat on the ground and pulled off her shoes and stockings and rubbed her feet, a frown pulling at her forehead. She'd never get used to such contraptions, she decided. It was bad enough wearing them in town, but here on the trail?

"Here," came her father's voice behind her, "put these on."

Looking around, she saw moccasins in his hands and nearly squealed with delight. Reaching up to take them from his hands, she smiled. Pa hadn't forgotten. He remembered she loved to feel wild and free. She was glad to shed the shoes she'd been forced to wear. For an instant the thought crossed her mind that Elizabeth wouldn't approve. Rachel quickly shrugged off the thought, for this was a different world and it suited her perfectly. Slipping her feet into the moccasins, she wiggled her toes as a smile widened her mouth.

Moving into the Gap of Clinch Mountain, the party passed by an abandoned station.

"What happened to the station, John?" Jacob asked as they passed by.

"Chief Benge of the Chickamauga Cherokee attacked it a couple of years ago. Everyone was killed except for a child who was taken into captivity." John gave Jacob a warning look. "But no need to let the rest know about that right now," John informed him. It was hard enough taking such a large party through. If the women became hysterical, it would be downright impossible.

Reaching the gap, Jane turned and looked east from where they had traveled. Her life in Wellington was *really* behind her now and her heart was filled with misgivings about leaving family behind. Teary-eyed, she had hemmed and hawed all morning whether to continue on or turn back.

A few times the temptation to leave was so great, that she found herself tugging the reins to turn around. She was sure she could make it if she left now. Caught up in such thoughts, she would dally until those behind her prodded her to move on ahead. Now it was too late. If she tried to leave now, when they were this far on their journey, Will would stop her. And even if he did allow her to go back, he would never let her take Jake. Not now. She gave Jake a quick squeeze, kissing the top of his head. No, she could leave Will, she could leave the Templeton family, she could leave all she knew in the party…but she couldn't leave Jake.

The party plodded on until mid-morning, stopping briefly for a noon meal.

Will hurried in to grab his johnnycake and jerked meat. Jane was jostling Jake, trying to console him. "Jake doesn't seem to feel well. He's crying a lot," Jane complained as Will, sitting on his haunches, began wolfing down his meal.

He looked appraisingly at the crying baby. "Probably just cutting teeth," he observed.

"I need you to help me, Will," she whined on the verge of tears.

"Can't," he answered through a mouthful of food. "I've got to tend to the herds." Looking at the storm passing over her face, he said, "Get Mother to help or one of the girls."

"They do help me. But I need *you*."

Standing up and grabbing the remains of his meal, he hurriedly seized his rifle and left. "I'm sorry, but I can't right now, Jane," were his parting words.

They rode up the valley of Little Moccasin Creek and down the valley to the mouth of Troublesome Creek. Travelers on the road usually avoided the Troublesome. For Troublesome was its name and troublesome it was.

Entering the Troublesome, Will, riding to the front of the line, asked apprehensively, "You sure this is the way, John?"

As difficult as the going would be, no thieves or Indians would be looking for them here since traveling parties no longer used this route. At least, that's what John Winslow was hoping, and he was staking the party's safety on that.

"We follow the creek-bed to the Clinch River ford," he said, his tone discouraging any further questions.

Without another word, Will kneed his horse around and rode back.

On either side of the creek, mountains rose up, dark, steep, and forbidding looking. The horses didn't like this creek. They balked when urged forward. Their hooves slipped and shifted on the wet rocks. Pitching forward, their loads shifted and sometimes landed in pools of water.

"Think Indians will attack us here?" Rachel whispered to Ransom.

Ransom quickly searched the mountainous terrain, searching for signs they might be lying in wait to strike.

John Winslow sat quietly on his horse studying the shore-line. The river twisted and growled over the rocks, but the ford of the Clinch River revealed that the crossing place wasn't much more than knee deep in most places. The river itself was dark and cold, hidden from sunlight by the trees.

144

They forded the creek on a shelf of rock just as the men came back from the hunt.

It was an especially hard day of travel since so many had gotten little sleep the night before. At last, the party crossed Clinch River and by nightfall everyone was ready for the day to be done.

CHAPTER TWENTY- FOUR

WEARY FROM THE DAY'S hard journey, the women in the Templeton camp spoke little as they unloaded the packhorses and prepared supper. The men returned from hobbling the horses and opening the clappers on the cattle.

"Here!" Jane said, as she thrust Jake at Will when he walked into the camp.

Taking the baby, he sat on the ground as Elizabeth brought his food.

Jane was becoming openly antagonistic toward Will, but the family held their tongue. As long as Will was willing to endure her hostility, there wasn't much they could do. But listening to her constant whining got tiring at times. When she started, they offered no opinion except knowing looks at one another.

John finally joined them as they were finishing up. Taking his food from Elizabeth, he flashed a smile and said, "Thanks, Mrs. Templeton."

All the Templeton men, John, and Sam were discussing the settling of Stone Valley and the communal raising of temporary cabins.

Jane, bending over the fire and stirring the pot, overheard their conversation and straightened up. She turned slowly toward them. "You mean to tell me," she said with astonishment, "I'm going to have to live in a cabin?"

"Only temporarily, Jane," Will said. "It will take a while for the lumber to be ready before we can build homes. We should be able to build by the winter, spring at the latest."

"I've never lived in a cabin in my life!" Jane said, anger flushing her face. "You never told me that this was part of the conditions that I would have to put up with, Will!"

"I supposed you knew that all along."

"Well…how would I know that? You talk to everyone else but me! I never thought coming to Kentucky would—would mean living in something that boorish backwoods people live in!"

Jane threw the spoon down and said, "I refuse! I'm not some country-bred illiterate brought up on a dirt floor!"

John's face flushed with anger at those remarks. He and Emily had raised Rachel in a cabin.

Will flashed a quick look at John. "Jane, cabins aren't anything unusual. The Germans and the Swedes have built and lived in cabins on the frontier. The Swedes built the first log cabins in America in their settlements around Delaware Bay in the early 1600's. Germans, coming later into Pennsylvania, did the same. And John and Rachel lived in a cabin, remember?"

Jane glanced at Rachel and sneered. "Yes, and look at her! Wild as an Indian when she came to live with Jacob and Elizabeth, upsetting the whole town with her ways! Brought nothing but trouble on all of us! So much trouble…that we had to leave Wellington!"

Jane pointed her finger at Rachel and giving her a withering look, said, "All of this is her fault…nobody but hers. If it wasn't for her, I'd still be back in Wellington with Mother and Father, instead of..." waving her hand around at the woods, "this—this God-forsaken place!"

The men jumped to their feet at her remarks, ready to defend Rachel. Will, holding the baby in one arm, stood between Jane and the men, palm forward, warding them off. "Jane, you owe an apology to everyone...especially John and Rachel," he threw over his shoulder.

Rachel's face had gone white. She sat in shock, blinking hard, and then tears began to fill her eyes. Elizabeth and Cissa looked with astonishment at Jane.

Like a bolt of lightning, Rachel was up and gone from the camp.

Jane folded her arms and raised her head defiantly. Everyone was concerned about Rachel and not her. Rachel this and Rachel that. Sometimes, it got to be like a bad taste in her mouth. A taste she wanted to spit out. Well, now she *did* spit it out, and as she looked at the disapproving faces around her, her own face began to fall, and she slowly uncrossed her arms, and said, "Well...."

"Rachel's gone!" Cissa cried, as she glanced toward the blackness of the forest.

Ransom swung around to where she had been sitting.

"Oh, no! Where did she go?" Jacob asked.

"Check the rest of the party," John snapped. "See if she's gone there."

Ransom looked around, terror striking his heart. "No," Ransom countered. "She won't be there. She's not afraid of the dark." He pointed to the woods. "She's out there somewhere."

John sprang into action. "Round up some men. We've got to find her."

Jacob put his hand on John's arm. "John, it's dark. You won't find her tonight. Wait until the light of day and then we'll send out search parties."

He shook off Jacob's hand. "For heaven's sake, Jacob, she's my daughter!" John exclaimed frantically. "I can't leave her out there by herself!" Quickly reaching for the cane that had been cut and binding together some stalks, he dipped the ends into the fire until they lit. "The rest of you can stay here," he growled, "but I'm leaving."

And with that said, he turned on his heel to leave.

"I'll go with you," Ransom said, keeping step with John.

"Same here," echoed Sam, his hand already reaching for his rifle.

"All right, I'll go too," said Will as James picked up his rifle to go.

"I hope you're satisfied, Jane," Will said between clenched teeth as he deposited Jake back into her arms.

"I'm going too, John," Jacob called.

John swung around. "No, Jacob. You stay here and protect the women. No point in everyone going."

The men left the camp and met with Gabe Roswell.

"What's all the ruckus?" Gabe questioned.

"Rachel's lost in the woods," Will called over his shoulder in an urgent voice, keeping pace with John and Ransom.

"What's she doing in the woods this time of night?" Gabe wanted to know.

"Long story," James told him as he hurried along.

"I'll go with you." Gabe's dogs knew something was up by the tone of his voice. Instantly alert, they began to bark and scuffle.

Getting out of sight of camp into the dark curtain of night, Gabe called, "Try to stick together and break off twigs or branches so we can find our way back."

"Rachel has some growing up to do, that's certain, but she's a good-hearted girl," thought Jacob after they had gone. "She's made Ransom a good wife. Come to think about it, it's not so much Rachel who needs to grow up, but Jane.*"*

Elizabeth and Cissa cleaned the supper dishes and prepared for bed, although it was doubtful that anyone would get much sleep.

"I didn't mean to sound so mean, really I didn't," Jane said contritely in the aftermath of her outburst.

The women were silent.

Mortified, Jane covered his face with a hand. "I'm sorry. I never meant to attack anyone." Looking up at Elizabeth, she pleaded, "Please don't put the freeze on me, Mother Templeton," Jane sobbed, as she dropped her head. "I can't stand that."

Elizabeth looked at Jane with a little sympathy on her face. She had known for some time that Jane was not happy. She had so hoped when William and Jane married that it would be a happy marriage. She knew William was ambitious and had his faults. Time and time again she nearly stepped in to help solve their problems. However, Jacob forbade her from interfering in their affairs. "They have to take care of their own troubles," he explained.

Maybe Will *was* a little too ambitious, but that was something he and Jane would have to work out in their own way and in their own time. With one child already and another on the way, it seemed all so complicated. Jane never really wanted to leave Wellington and no one knew what it would take to make her satisfied with Stone Valley. To Elizabeth, all that lay ahead for their marriage was trouble.

"Please, Elizabeth," Jane begged as she stretched out her hand. "I'm asking again. Don't freeze me out."

Being an emotional person, and at times acting accordingly, this was one of the few times that Elizabeth actually spoke out of thoughts that were drawn deep. "I don't mean to, Jane," she said quietly. "It's just that you hurt Rachel very much."

With a resigned sigh, she continued, "Rachel's never meant any harm to anyone. Her ways have been a little different from ours, but all of God's children are different in some respect. She's been through so much, Jane. You know that."

Elizabeth gave Jane a sharp look. "I would work very hard to win her friendship back, if I were you."

Jane shook her head in agreement. "You're right. I know you're right. I don't know if she'll ever feel the same toward me again, but I'm willing to try."

Elizabeth smiled slightly. "Rachel's a very forgiving person. You must remember though, you ground dirt into some wounds of hers. She's having a hard time with her past, though she doesn't talk about it. It takes gentleness and love to win her. I think you'll find that's the cross you will have to bear."

Jane tucked Jake into the tent, careful not to wake him. She had not prayed for a long time, so unhappy she had been. She thought and thought and then finally spilled out a few words. "Lord, forgive me of my sins. I've been a miserable wretch. Help me to be a better wife. Forgive me for the words I spoke to Rachel and— and help me win back her friendship."

Settling onto the blanket by Jake, she quickly sat up again and folding her hands in prayer, "Protect her in the dark out there and bring her back safely."

CHAPTER TWENTY-FIVE

RACHEL STUMBLED THROUGH THE THICK FOREST, blindly pushing her way around and through the trees, disregarding the scraping of her skin and an occasional rip in her clothes, tears flowing down her face as she went.

"'Wild as an Indian' she called me. Caused trouble for everyone. Made everyone leave Wellington? How was that my fault? How could Jane speak that way about me? I thought she liked me and was my friend."

Finally, overtaken with exhaustion, she stopped running and fell to the ground. She lay there for a long time, her face pressed into the pungent, rotting leaves.

Calming down and turning her head to one side, she rubbed the flecks of spiny leaves from her face with the palm of her hand. For a few, hurting minutes, she couldn't think. A terrible heaviness, a weightiness that defied any rational thought, cloaked her. She was tired. Tired of criticism and tired of thinking anymore. When would she ever escape the censure of others?

With a shudder, she recalled destructive gossip of others in Wellington that hissed like the forked tongue of a snake. Disapproval followed her everywhere, like an ever-lengthening shadow. It was there in Wellington and it followed her here on the road to Kentucky.

Turning over on her back and stretching out her arms, she lay for a long time in the darkness, listening to the sound of her breathing, concentrating on her chest moving rhythmically up and down as she inhaled and exhaled. Her head turned as the shriek of a distant panther stiffened her limbs into motionlessness, and she squeezed her eyes shut. Her nerves became taut again and almost cracked as the shriek was repeated. Addled that she had run because of Jane's accusation, it dawned on her in hindsight that this was Indian country.

"Was that the call of an Indian?" she asked herself, her thoughts racked with fright.

How still the night air was! The slightest sounds were magnified in her uneasy and alert ears. Being alone out here, she felt like someone was close by, peering at her, watching her every move.

"I've really done it this time," she thought, "out of the frying pan into the fire. I wish I'd stayed put and borne the brunt of her words."

Her eyes blinked hard, trying to will the light of the moon to appear through the massive trees, so that she could see through the thick canopy of darkness. The melancholy moan of an owl spiraled through the air, bouncing off the trees. Rising up slowly on one arm, her eyes rolled from side to side, watching for any movement—as if she could see anything at all in the blackness. She breathed short, shallow breaths, as the stillness of the night, and the fear of Indians, threatened to completely envelope her.

"I can't think about Indians now," she told herself. "I'll get scared again if I think about them."

There were no more cries, all was quiet again, and she willed herself to relax.

"I'm getting spooked," she thought. "I've never been afraid of the dark before." Drawing a deep breath, she gave a shaky laugh.

"Caused trouble, have I?" Sanity began to wash over her and she pushed herself to a sitting position.

"I suppose they're out looking for me now. Guess I'm causing trouble again. Always running away, I am. Well, I'd better head back toward camp before I cause a bigger fuss than I have."

She struggled to her feet and brushed the unseen crushed leaves from her clothes.

She was lost. Twisting this way and that, she searched for the light of campfires but saw none. The forest hid most of the moonlight that was out. Only an occasional trickle filtered through the tall trees. She turned back to where she thought she had come from and began to walk in the darkness, only guessing she might be headed the right way.

Suddenly, the ground gave way beneath her and she found herself tumbling down into rock. Hitting a solid wall, she came to a halt. After a few moments she sat up.

"Ooh!" Rubbing her face where it hurt, she licked her lower lip and tasted blood.

She kept silent, listening for any movement. Hearing nothing, she tried to stand up, but could only stoop. She felt the wall and discovered she had tumbled into a small cave.

"Well, at least no Indians will find me here," she thought sourly and sat down again to ponder her situation. She had been ensconced in the little cave for some time when she heard dogs barking.

"Rachel! Rachel!"

Someone was calling her name. She scrambled on all fours, attempting to stand up best she could.

"Rachel!"

She gulped once and found her voice. "Here! I'm over here!" her echoing voice shouted.

"Rachel?"

"Is that you, Pa?"

"Rachel?" sounded Ransom's voice.

"Ransom?" Rachel asked, at the sound of his voice.

"Keep talking, Rachel, until we find you," he instructed.

She kept up a stream of words and soon heard the rustling of leaves near the mouth of the cave.

"You're getting closer. I can hear you," she yelled. "Over here."

"Keep talking," John ordered.

"Be careful when you get here," she shouted. "I fell into a cave."

"This way, Gabe," she heard Sam's voice shout over the din of the barking dogs.

Holding the torch high over his head, John shoved aside the underbrush. Trampling it down and handing the torch to Ransom, he leaned down at the mouth of the cave. Rachel stared wide-eyed up at him, her dark hair snarled and tangled.

"Pa!" she called, relieved.

"Rachel!" Looking for a few seconds, John said, "The cave's not too terribly deep." Dropping to the ground and lying flat on his belly, he reached an arm down to her. "Can you take hold of my hand?"

Galvanized by the authority in his voice, "Yes, Pa," she answered. Rachel fumbled for his hand. At her touch, John grabbed her wrist, pulled, then pushing himself to his knees, lifted her up, scraping her along the wall as she came.

Rachel, with effort, lifted her head on an aching neck. "Pa! Oh, Pa!" she cried tearfully, thankful she had been found. She wrapped her arms around him and was never so glad to see anyone in her life.

"Rachel, are you all right?" Ransom asked as he knelt down, handing the torch back to John, and reaching out to her.

She moved into his good arm and said, "Ransom! Yes—yes, I'm fine. I think I've bloodied my face though." Running her hands over her skirt, "And I've torn my clothes."

The rest of the men followed John's torch until they happened upon the cave.

"Watch out," John cautioned. "There are caves around here."

"Blackest I've ever seen it," Sam observed. "I don't think we can find our way back tonight. We'll be swallowed up by the forest for sure."

"We'll head back at first light," Gabe decided. "That way we can follow the markings we left."

John was relieved and angry at the same time. With faint annoyance wrinkling his forehead, he said, "If you were younger, Rachel, I'd turn you over my knee."

Running his fingers through his hair, he scolded, "You can't go running off every time someone does or says something you don't like. You've got to learn, girl, this is no way to behave. That's life. Not everybody is going to like what you do or say and it's time to face the facts and learn that. You're no longer a child."

She wished the night would hide her blushing face. Pa had never turned her over his knee in his life and now he was talking to her like this, right in front of everyone. And they were all staring at her. If she could, she would disappear into the blackness of the cave again.

"I know, Pa," she mumbled as she lowered her head. "I'm sorry I caused you all so much trouble."

It was clear he was agitated. "You've got the whole camp upset by now. They'll wonder where we are and if Indians have captured us. Nobody will get any sleep."

"I didn't think, Pa."

"That's obvious," he stated, none too graciously.

Will cleared his throat. "Rachel, I want to say right off, that I'm sorry for the things Jane said. I want you to know the rest of us don't feel that way."

"Thank you, Will," said Rachel, gratefully. "I—I…." She shook her head as her words died.

Ransom propped himself against the opening of the cave. At least it was cool here with the air of the cave drifting up. The men sat on the ground and debated whether to build a fire, but that idea was soon forgotten as their talk turned to Stone Valley again. The dogs settled down as soft conversation was heard among the men.

Ransom drew Rachel close to him.

"Rachel, don't ever do that again," he scolded her softly. "I was nearly sick with worry about you, wondering if Indians got to you out here."

"Well, I'm glad you're here with me now, Ransom," she replied as she leaned her head on his shoulder. "Oh, Ransom, I was so afraid," she whispered frantically. "I've never been afraid of the dark before, but it was horrible—so horrible! I didn't know where I was and I heard the scream of a panther and didn't know if it was an Indian or not."

He pulled her closer and wished his other arm was free from its sling.

Ransom was so still, and hearing his even breathing, Rachel thought he had drifted off to sleep. She started when he broke the silence.

"Don't let what Jane said bother you," he said.

But it did. More than anyone could know. And she wondered, "Did Jane merely voice what others thought?" The idea filled her with fear and worry again. She moved slightly in the crook of his arm.

"Ransom?"

"Yes?"

"Do I—do I seem that way to you?" Rachel asked uncertainly. "Always causing trouble, I mean."

Ransom smiled in the darkness. When he had left for the university, he had thought he could never love her with more intensity than he did at that moment. But now, knowing her as his wife, his emotions were sharpened with the passion that intimacy brings.

Oh, he'd tried to convince himself that it was in her best interest that he had prodded her into becoming what he thought was proper...proper dress and proper manners, things that mattered to others and had nothing to do with who or what she was. His mind swept back to the time that she first came to live at the parsonage. A somewhat wild child she was, with hair that tumbled freely down her shoulders. Even now, she refused to wear a cap and only donned a hat when the sun was beating down upon her with its hottest glare.

His mother had a difficult time convincing Rachel to wear a corset. She still didn't like it and complained about it from time to time. He was sure there were days she didn't wear one. She never really belonged in Wellington, nor had any wish to. The ways of society did not impress her, where everyone seemed to be cast from the same mold. Everyone knew what to expect from everyone else as they all followed the same rules of etiquette. He'd been torn between allowing her to be herself and pushing her to become what others expected of her. City life was not for her. This rugged life, with its adventure and uncertainty, suited her better.

However, he had never liked uncertainty. An ordered life, arranged to his liking, was more his style.

Rachel could never quite become one of them or even like him, for that matter. Too much of herself had been forged on the farm, in her own world of carefree abandonment, and in the wide free world of nature. She recognized and accepted the differences of those around her, but could not be pushed to become a replica of any of them, and would never surrender her own sense of self.

When he didn't speak for several moments, she asked the question again.

"Some people think trouble is anything different from what they are used to," he said thoughtfully.

"You didn't really answer me," she persisted.

"Well—you've just got your own ways," he answered diplomatically. "And there are those that let that trouble them."

"But why should that trouble them?" she questioned.

"It's hard to explain. People like things to fit into their own way of thinking. It's like trying to put a big, square peg into a round hole. It can't be done and that's why they're troubled."

"So…you still didn't answer me. Am I always causing trouble?"

"Not deliberately," he hedged.

"So you're saying I do," she insisted.

"Get that bee out of your bonnet and get some sleep," Ransom said, giving her a little shake, considering the subject closed.

She giggled. He knew she didn't wear a bonnet.

He couldn't stifle the yawn that suddenly overtook him. "We have a long day tomorrow," he said drowsily.

CHAPTER TWENTY- SIX

AN HOUR AFTER THE SUN ROSE, they entered the camp next morning.

Hearing their voices, Elizabeth rose from where she had been sitting in sleep outside the tent. Her eyes were circled and tired, her face drawn, for she had not slept much.

Jane had wanted to give her mother-in-law some kind of comfort throughout the night. She wanted to say, "Don't worry. Rachel can find her way back." But she knew better than to say anything at all. Somehow she needed to convince Elizabeth that she really wasn't so awful. But the deed was over and done, and think as she would, Jane saw no way to rectify what had already been said.

"Thank God you found her!" Elizabeth whispered in a voice of relief, and rushed to give Rachel an embrace. Reaching up to touch her cheek, "My dear, you've hurt your face!"

"I tumbled into a cave," Rachel said with an impish grin. "I scraped it and I guess I bit my lip when I fell in."

"No time to waste," John's voice rang out. "Grab a quick breakfast, get packed up, attend to the herds, and let's head out. We need to cross the Clinch River today."

Jane held her hand out towards Will, but he did not speak and quickly brushed by her. As none of the men acknowledged her, Jane gave a fleeting, pitiful look at Rachel in Elizabeth's arms. *She* now felt like the outcast and it was a gritty feeling in her mouth.

Gabe walked into the camp and was met by Abigail.

"What happened last night? Why were you gone all night?" she asked, concern written all over her face.

He beamed a wide grin. "Noticed, did you?"

She drew herself up. "Of course. But to be sure," she said dismissively, "it's none of my business."

As she turned to go, he took her arm. "Don't get miffed. One of the Templeton women got herself lost in the forest."

"Which one?"

He released her arm.

"Rachel."

"What was she doing out in the forest at night?"

He shrugged. "Who knows?"

"Well...I've got you some breakfast ready."

"Thanks. Be right there."

In spite of her father's disapproval, Gabe was taking all his meals with them now. She had hinted at religious talk, but he wasn't sure he was ready to talk about that...not just yet.

∞∞∞∞∞∞∞∞∞∞∞∞∞∞∞

The following morning they set out across the ford of Stock Creek. Following the trail, they crossed the creek six times and here the hard mountain travel began. The path followed the creek in a torturous, steep climb over the north end of Stock Creek Ridge.

As the climb became steeper, the riders dismounted to lead their horses up the ascent to the ridge, tugging at them as they balked going forward.

Climbing up the ridge, Jane precariously scaled the mountain, her feet slipping on small stones easily dislodged by a foot. Gripping the howling Jake firmly, she vowed for the hundredth time that day, "If we make it through this alive, I'll make Will Templeton pay for this! I never wanted to come on this fool-hardy trip anyway!"

As the animals drew back from the steep incline, they were prodded by young and old to continue when they halted. From all over the party shouts of "Haw! Get along there!" could be heard. Losing their footing and pitching forward, some of the horses lost the goods packed in their baskets and the party was forced to stop more than once for someone to retrieve and repack their loads.

"How are you bearing up, Rachel?" Ransom asked as he stopped momentarily, slightly winded.

"Don't mind me, Ransom. I can make it. You've got the horses to lead." She found that moving very quickly on the rocks tore her moccasins. "It's back to shoes after today," she told him.

Jacob and Elizabeth were in the front of the party. As Elizabeth panted, she remarked to Jacob with a half-laugh, "Whew! I didn't feel old before, but believe me, I feel it now."

"You can make it, dear, I know you can," Jacob said.

"Oh, there's no doubt about that. I just wish I wasn't wearing this corset. One thing about it Jacob, there's no room for proprieties here. It's getting packed away along with etiquette in the morning!"

"That's my Lizzy!"

A smile touched her lips. "You haven't called me that in years."

"You know, this journey kind of reminds me of our earlier years together...hard times."

Elizabeth considered this for a moment, looking thoughtful. She supposed they had fallen into the trap that sometimes accompanies success. Jacob had been dissatisfied for a long time...that she readily acknowledged. In spite of his achievement of building one of the most flourishing churches in the county, he was essentially, a down-to-earth man with one simple desire, to please his God. Day by day, she had watched as his youth seemed to be renewed here on the road.

The party reached the highest point, Horton's Summit. When everyone had assembled there, John announced they would camp there for the night.

Descending the mountain would prove to be more difficult he told them. "The going down will be just as steep," he warned the weary travelers. "Watch for those coming down behind you. They could sweep you with them should they fall."

The expanse of the mountains was overwhelming. The blue of the peaks faded into gray and then black. Mountains everywhere! It seemed endless! For Jane, this seemed like a final farewell to the life she'd left behind. No going back now. She was feeling tired and nauseated with pregnancy. Will walked up to her and handed her a cup of water and some cheese Elizabeth had unpacked.

"Here. This will help some."

"How did you—?"

He gave her a knowing smile. "I know." Taking Jake from her, he said, "You rest. I'll take care of Jake."

Tears came to her eyes. This was the first time in months that she felt any real tenderness from him, especially after her last outburst. She'd tried to be good since that night, really she had.

"Thanks," she offered gratefully, and after eating, she stretched out for a long nap.

Nathan Hargrave brought out his fiddle, but no one was in the mood for dancing. He played a lively melody at first, but soon switched to a soulful tune. It was soothing as his bow drew across the strings, making them feel they hadn't completely lost touch with civilization.

CHAPTER TWENTY- SEVEN

THE NEXT DAY the party made its descent down the mountain into a little valley. This basin led the party along a buffalo trail until they came to Little Flat Lick, a marshy field where the spring's minerals caked the surrounding soil and where game came from miles away for the salty ooze.

"We'll camp here for the night," John directed.

John gathered a few of the men together and informed them that rogues and thieves were known to frequent the area. "Keep an eye out tonight for anything out of the ordinary. Pass it on through the camp."

But Robert and the others in the back of the party didn't get the message. Late, that evening, two men rode up to the end of the party where Robert and Cordelia were camped.

"Get down and rest your saddle," Robert invited. "You men hungry?"

They stepped down and taking their rifles, held them across the front of their chests.

A beefy, greasy sort of man, with dark hair and in his thirties, appeared to be the leader of the two. Citing his name as Caleb

Hogue, he introduced the other man as Fallon Brossart, his cousin. Brossart was a nervous type, with a red face splotched with pimples. They both were shabbily dressed with torn breeches and leggings and a brooding look on their faces.

"We got no money to offer you," Hogue said.

"No matter," said Robert cheerfully. "It's nothing fancy. But we'll share what we've got."

Keeping his rifle in hand, Hogue grunted and then sat down cross-legged by the fire while Brossart shifted on his feet. "Sit down, Fallon!" Hogue barked. Brossart did as he was told and immediately dropped to the ground.

Cordelia threw Robert a cautious look, but Robert took no notice. She kept Starr in her arms and drew Adam close to her skirts. She didn't like the looks of these men. Not that their attire was any different than some that they encountered along the way, but she didn't like the way they kept eyeing her and their tent. The thought crossed her mind to go to the Dickson camp, but she was afraid to leave Robert alone with the men.

"Where you folks headed?" asked Hogue nonchalantly.

"We're moving to Green River Country, Kentucky," Robert answered. "Maybe you've heard of it? A place called Stone Valley."

Hogue shook his head no.

"We're settling a community in that area."

"Is that so," Hogue commented. "Where'd you hail from?"

"Virginia."

"What's your occupation?"

The question wasn't too unusual, but just having met the man, it struck Robert as odd.

"I was in banking," he revealed cautiously.

Hogue settled himself against a fallen log. Keeping his voice even-toned, he inquired, "Is that so?"

"Yes," Robert admitted.

Hogue looked at the pot over the fire.

Robert took notice and said, "Cordelia, get these men some food."

Throwing Robert a frown, she considered these men unwelcome, but reluctantly got two pewter plates and filled them.

They ate hungrily without speaking or looking at Robert and Cordelia. Inquisitive, Robert asked where they came from.

Shrugging his shoulders without looking up, Hogue answered, "Nowhere special."

Robert grew quiet. Looking Cordelia's way, he began to feel uneasy about these men and silently willed them to finish their meal and be on their way. The unspoken message in Cordelia's eyes said she thought the same.

The silence stretched uncomfortably as no one spoke for a few minutes. "What are they up to?" Robert pondered. "There's plenty of game around. No reason they should be hungry."

When their plates were empty, Hogue and Brossart rose wordlessly, and with a last glance at the tent, stepped up onto their horses. With a nod to Robert, and a flick of the reins, they slowly and quietly rode away.

CHAPTER TWENTY-EIGHT

RACHEL, JANE, AND CISSA were sitting at the edge of the clearing, taking their supper meal, and catching a breeze that had blown up. After the meal, Rachel took her precious pack of needles and some thread and concentrated on mending a tear in her skirt that had caught on a bramble—not much torn, but it should be sewn right away since she had only a few clothes with her.

Behind her, a teasing voice asked, "Tear your skirt on our climb today, did you?" Looking up, she saw Sam peering over her shoulder. They had not spoken since the blockhouse and the baiting tone of his voice irritated her.

Hot words simmered to her lips and with difficulty she checked them. Instead, she frowned and didn't answer. It wouldn't do for Jane and Cissa to discover the contention between her and Sam, nor the reason. Turning back to her sewing, she jabbed and stuck her finger with the needle. Drawing her brows together, she put her pricked finger in her mouth.

Cissa looked at Rachel, puzzled at Rachel's reaction. "Rachel," she said, "Sam is speaking to you."

He squatted down on his haunches. "Here, let me see," holding out his hand to her.

Reluctantly, she held her hand out for his inspection.

"Not very good at mending, I see," he observed with a hint of laughter in his voice and the impudence of it galled her.

She wanted to pull her hand back, but Cissa and Jane were staring at her. He was laughing at her and she dared not confront him about it, not in front of them anyway. Blushing from anger, she retorted hotly, "Stitching has not been my best subject, if you *must* know, Mr. Spencer."

Grinning, Sam tossed her hand into her lap. "Maybe these ladies could teach you how," he said as he stood up and walked away, chuckling to himself.

"That was rather rude of you, Rachel, not to answer Sam like that," upbraided Cissa.

"I'd have been a sight ruder if he and I had been alone," Rachel thought and put her head down and continued with her sewing.

"I must confess, as much as I love you," Cissa said in an exasperated tone, "you're hard to figure out sometimes."

The climb had been difficult and her moccasins were badly torn. They were, she decided, beyond repair. She had no awl to repair them so she laid them aside.

A rifle was placed on the ground and Rachel looked up as John sat down beside her.

She smiled. "Hi, Pa."

He lifted a moccasin from her side. "I don't think you'll be able to repair those. Maybe I have another solution." He reached inside his shirt and pulled out two more.

"Oh, Pa!" she cried gleefully, took them, and immediately put them on. "How'd you know I needed another pair?"

"I may be busy, girl, but I still keep an eye on you. You can't come on a journey like this without extra moccasins. I just stopped in for my meal. Be a good daughter and go fetch it for me."

"Are things progressing along well, Mr. Winslow?" Cissa asked.

"Oh, to be sure. Had a little incident a while ago, though. One of the horses choked on some cane leaves. We had to wrestle it to the ground so that we could pour water down its throat and wash down the clump of leaves. The horse is all right and should be ready for travel tomorrow."

"How dreadful!" Jane declared.

He shrugged. "Those things just happen."

"I suppose so," she said, her voice trailing off.

John lay back against a tree and closing his eyes, fell immediately into a light sleep. Awakened by Rachel's footsteps, he apologized to the girls. "Sorry for drifting off like that. My sleep is often interrupted during the night."

Rachel was carrying ham and cheese and a cup of fresh milk.

"Um…that looks good. I could go for some biscuits about now."

"All we've got is clap-bread Pa," Rachel remarked.

"Reminds me of the Israelites when they left Canaan," John said good-naturedly.

"How is that, Mr. Winslow?" Jane inquired.

"They had to eat clap-bread too," he answered between bites. "You know—unleavened bread. These women teach you how to make biscuits, Rachel?" he asked.

"Oh, yes, Mr. Winslow," Cissa beamed him a bright smile. "Rachel is becoming quite a good cook."

"Yes, she certainly is," agreed Jane.

"I'm only so-so, Pa," Rachel contradicted sourly.

"Her mother was one of the best cooks I knew," John proudly volunteered.

"So Rachel told us," said Jane.

"You ladies holding up?" John asked as he bit into the chunk of ham.

"Yes," Jane answered as she rubbed the back of her neck, "but I tire so easily these days."

"I do too," echoed Cissa, "I guess it's because…." she broke off, embarrassed that she nearly talked about her pregnancy to John. It would not do to discuss delicate matters such as having babies with this large, imposing man. She rose and she and Jane busied themselves with the cleanup of the supper utensils. Of course, it was well known throughout the camp that the Templeton girls were pregnant. The corner of John's mouth curved up at their embarrassment.

Rachel put aside her sewing and laid back on the ground with her knees drawn up, one leg crossed and dangling over the other. She placed one arm casually across her stomach and looked up toward the tops of the trees. "You know, Pa," she began as she swatted at a swarm of gnats, "I've been feeling tired more quickly than normal. My stomach doesn't feel so good, either. Do you think I might be coming down with something?"

With his hand poised in mid-air to lift the cup to his lips, he turned and looked at her, his eyes drifting to her stomach. Could she be expecting, too? Was it possible that this free-spirited daughter of his would become a mother? Visions of a dark-haired boy flitted through his mind, a boy that he could hunt and fish with. A grandson. Yes, he relished the thought of that.

"I don't know, girl," said John, speculation in his eyes, and then took a drink. Setting his cup on the ground thoughtfully, "Why don't you talk to the doctor?" he asked.

She hesitated. "Well—I don't know. I—I guess I'll be fine," she reflected as she rubbed her stomach. "Just need to get more sleep.

After all, it's been some rough going. Sure," she nodded her head, "that's all it is."

He shrugged and feigned indifference. "Do as you please," said John as he finished off his meal.

But he was smiling as he said it.

CHAPTER TWENTY-NINE

TOM WAS WORRIED. Robert and Cordelia's baby, Starr, had awakened him with her crying and he climbed out of his tent to investigate. Walking into their camp he found that Robert and Cordelia were not in their tent, and Tom, reaching across sleeping Adam, picked the baby up and tried to hush her. She wouldn't be quieted and he glanced toward the dark. "Probably just went to use the necessary," he thought. But as he waited, they didn't return. The baby's cries woke Lacy, and finding Tom gone, she climbed out and made her way into Robert's camp.

"Where are Robert and Cordelia?" Lacy asked sleepily as she took the baby from Tom, putting her against her shoulder and patting her on the back.

"I don't know." Tom's eyes were drawn to the provisions in the tent. Something was wrong. They looked ransacked. Kneeling down at the tent door and crawling inside, he searched for Robert's sack of gold coins. It was gone!

Walking two camps up and waking George and Margaret, Tom returned and gave his rifle to Lacy. "If some stranger comes, don't hesitate to use this. Your parents are coming and I'm going to the front for John Winslow."

As he made his way through the party toward John, Gabe's dogs roused and began to growl softly. Coming awake instantly, he saw Tom weaving quietly through the myriad of tents.

"Something wrong, Tom?" Gabe asked, alerted.

"I don't know, Gabe. Robert and Cordelia are missing. Their provisions have been ransacked and Robert's money taken. I'm going for John Winslow. If you don't mind, go take care of Lacy 'till I get back."

Gabe grabbed his rifle and with his dogs following, took off for the end of the camp.

John woke instantly at the sound of Tom's footsteps.

"What's going on, McClelland?"

"Can't say for sure, John. Robert and Cordelia are missing and Robert's gold is gone."

Sam and Frank came awake and were instantly out of their tents and on their feet.

Will and James, standing front guard, heard the commotion in the camp and left their posts.

"The McClellands are missing," John explained. "You men have to stay on guard. Sam, Frank, Tom, and I will take care of this."

Arriving at Robert's tent, John appraised the situation.

"How long have they been gone?" he asked.

"Don't rightly know," Tom answered. "The baby woke me with her crying."

Hearing the noise of voices, the men on rear guard came into the camp.

"What about you men on duty. Have you seen McClelland and his wife? Have you seen anything at all?"

"Nothing," they said, shaking their heads. "The cattle and horses have been a little restless tonight, though."

They were close to the canebrake. Cutting several cane and tying them together, John made a torch for the search.

Following the water in the marsh, John found an opening where someone had trodden the cane down. Going into the brake, it was not long before he found what he had desperately hoped he would not see.

Two bodies that didn't move.

They were dead.

They were also Robert and Cordelia.

As the other men were close on his heels, John yelled over his shoulder, "Tell Tom to stay back."

Frank looked over to what had caught John's eye and spotted the dead bodies whose scalps had been split open by a hatchet. Setting himself between that gruesome sight and Tom, Frank swung around to hold Tom back.

Passive at first, it took only a moment for Tom to figure out that something was terribly wrong.

"Get outta my way," Tom yelled, and with a grunting sound, he wrestled loose. Pushing his way to where John stood, Tom was filled with horror as he saw his brother mutilated by some unknown assailant.

Dropping his rifle, he grasped both sides of his head and gave an animal cry. Falling to the water, he wept loudly, refusing any efforts by the men to pull him away.

Like the toppling of a house of cards, from the rear to the front, the camps roused at the cries. Fearing Indians, men grabbed their rifles and the women huddled in the tents with the children.

The men gathered together and the word was passed quickly through the party, that Robert and Cordelia McClelland had been murdered.

Their corpses were brought to the edge of the camp and covered with blankets. Their bodies had been stripped of clothing and mutilated.

"Who could have done this, John? Indians?" Will asked.

"Nope. Warn't Indians," interjected Gabe. "It was somebody trying to make it look like Indian work."

He spat on the ground. "Appears to me it was thieves."

"Must have been watching us since we made camp," George Dickson said thoughtfully.

"I'd say they'd been watching us long before that," John remarked, "probably before we started up the ridge."

"And I'd say we should head out in the morning and pick up their trail," suggested Frank, not taking his eyes off the covered bodies.

"I can't leave the party," John said. "But if some of the rest of you want to, it's your decision. Remember, you'll need someone to guard your families and herds while you're gone. And if I were you, I'd go calm them down now."

The men shifted and began to shuffle toward their camps.

John didn't like to appear hard-hearted, but this was life on the frontier. Things happen. You move on.

"Double the guard," he directed. "I don't expect we'll have any more trouble out of them, seeing that we're on to them. The rest get as much sleep as you can. We'll bury the McClellands in the morning and then head out. George, you go back and comfort Tom as best as you can."

"Uncle Tom, where's Daddy and Mommy?" three-year-old Adam asked.

Taking the child in his arms, Tom said, "Daddy and Mommy are in Heaven. They want me and Lacy to be your daddy and mommy now. Do you understand?"

"No," Adam replied and began to cry. He tried to pull away out of Tom's arms. "I want Daddy."

"I know, son, I know."

Looking over Adam's head, his hand stroking the boy's brown curls, Tom studied Lacy holding Starr in her arms, his thoughts in turmoil. Without consulting her, he had declared to his nephew that they were now his new parents. An apology was in his soft, brown eyes, but before long, relief wiped away his misgivings at her look...a look that went far beyond words. A look that was as soft as his, filled with love for him and the children. They were their responsibility now. Hers and Tom's.

Jacob, as he had so many times before in funeral services, spoke the appropriate words of John 14:1: *Let not your heart be troubled: ye believe in God, believe also in me.*

As he elaborated on the fact that it is appointed unto man to die, Tom couldn't help thinking that Robert and Cordelia had died before their God-appointed time. Tom had no family but Lacy now. Oh, he had some distant cousins in Virginia, but his father, mother, and two sisters had passed away and now his only brother, Robert.

Robert's children would not forget their parents. Tom would make sure of that. He never imagined when he started this trip that in a short while he would be married and become the caretaker of two very young children.

CHAPTER THIRTY

NO SOONER HAD THEY BROKEN CAMP the next morning when two men rode in on horseback. One was short with a stocky build, the other tall and lanky.

Word quickly reached John of their arrival.

"Surely, it isn't the killers of last night," John thought. "They wouldn't be so brazen as to show their faces. Not in broad daylight, anyway."

He kneed his horse around and rode as swiftly as he could to get to the visitors, dodging livestock.

When John reached the back of the party, he slowed his horse and approached the men warily.

The only thing running through his mind was that if these men were the killers of the McClellands, they wouldn't hesitate to murder again. While he could take care of himself, he didn't want anyone else in the party caught in the crossfire.

"Can I help you, men?" John asked warily, his hand on his rifle.

"You be the head of this here party?" The short man asked, a fresh wad of tobacco puffing out his cheek.

"I am," answered John.

Looking around and sizing things up, "Seems like a good-sized party," he said.

Tension crackled, and something in John's gut told him that these men were not intent on joining the caravan. His eyes narrowed at the men.

That look didn't escape the stranger.

"We're not here to give you any problems, if that's what you're thinking. Your name?"

"Winslow," John finally offered.

"Like I said," he said with a nod, "we're not here to cause trouble."

"Good. First, let's start with why you *are* here."

"You got a man from South Carolina in this party by the name of Newgate?"

"Could be," John said, as his back stiffened. He drew his rifle and crossed it in front of him.

"Easy, now," cautioned the stranger, holding up an empty hand. "We're from Charleston. Charleston, South Carolina, that is. Name's Bill Sweeney and," pointing to the tall man, "this here is Wayne Carlton. We've been deputized by the authorities to bring Newgate back."

Pausing to spit a stream of juice, he continued, "Seems that he took off with some money stolen from some very influential citizens."

John sat astride his horse, absorbing that bit of information quietly, looking from Sweeney to Carlton. Nobody was taking anyone from the party without the necessary documents.

His set his mouth in a firm line and asked, "Have you got anything confirming that?"

"Sure have," said Sweeney, dismounting his horse. He opened his pack and withdrew a packet. "All legal." Unwrapping the outer covering, "It's all there," he added as he offered the papers to John.

Reaching down and taking them, John scanned them quickly. A dark scowl crossed his face and he looked again at Sweeney.

"All right, you stay here." John lifted the reins, preparing to turn, "I'll go get him."

Sweeney grabbed hold of the reins. "Not preparing to go and warn Newgate are you, friend?" he asked suspiciously, as his yellow teeth bared in a contemptuous smile.

John's jaw clenched. "I'll give you about five seconds to let go of my horse...*friend.*"

Sweeney's other hand slid bit by bit down toward his pistol and giving John a long, steady look through guarded eyes, he slowly released the reins.

Reining his horse around, John rode to Cabot Newgate's section of the party.

"Newgate! Got some men here to see you!" he called.

A puzzled look swept across Cabot's pudgy face, but was soon replaced with fear.

"Someone to see me?"

Noticing his discomfiture, Abigail asked, "Father? Who would want to see you out here in this wilderness?"

Sweeney and Carlton rode up, their hands on their pistols.

Cabot's first impulse was to slap the reins and escape. Looking around frantically, it didn't take long to dawn on him that there was nowhere to hide and he slumped in his saddle.

"Well, Sweeney...I wondered if someone would be after me," he remarked. "Guess it didn't work, after all."

"No, it didn't, Newgate. You're coming back with us, and if you don't mind, we'll take that precious cargo in your saddlebag...*and* your firearms."

When he cared to, or if it was important enough, Newgate could charm his way through most trouble. And right now, it was very important.

"Now, Sweeney," he began, flashing an affable smile.

Sweeney threw up a hand again.

"Save it, Newgate. I'm not one of your wenches."

A devious smile lit Cabot's face.

"We could strike a deal. What say...half for me and half for you...and Carlton."

Carlton's eyes lit with anticipation. "Hey, Sweeney. That's sounds like a pretty good—"

"Stop it, Carlton!" Sweeney's eyes flashed fire. "I'm not gonna be on the run like him.

"I'm not your business partner, either," Sweeney addressed Newgate. "Hand it over," he said, his hand outstretched.

Cabot glanced at Sweeney and, feeling less sure, decided not to challenge him. He'd had several run-ins with him in Charleston and could tell by the look in Sweeney's eyes that he was at the end of his patience. With a sigh, he reached around into his saddlebag, carefully pulled out a sack, and tracing the markings on the bag with his hand as gently as though it contained fragile china, handed it to Sweeney.

Taking the sack, searching the contents, then stowing it in his saddlebag, Sweeney turned and glared with contempt.

"Now...them firearms."

"I don't know," Cabot began dubiously, "I'd like to make sure Abigail will be protected. If you don't mind, I'd like to leave my rifle and pistol with my daughter."

"Father? What's he talking about…you going back? And why are Mr. Sweeney and Mr. Carlton here?"

With an arrogant smile on his face, Sweeney said, "I regret to tell you, Miss Newgate, your father is not—"

"I'll tell her myself, Sweeney," Cabot interrupted harshly.

Turning to Abigail, Cabot apologetically held out his hand to her. "Abby, I know you came here against your will. This coming to Kentucky was my idea. I can't expect you to ever forgive me, but one thing I do ask, please don't forget me. I did all this for you. I wanted you to find the happiness that you would never have found in Charleston. I wanted you to live in grand style, getting the recognition and acceptance you deserve. I thought taking the money from them and coming to Kentucky would give us both a new start."

"A new start?" she asked amazed. "You stole money? But, Papa, what you did was wrong!"

"I know, I know." He shook his head. "I can't expect you to understand."

Her mind twirled around and around trying to assimilate what he'd said. A determined look crossed her face.

"Then I'm going back with you," she stated, preparing to rein her horse around.

He held up his hand. "No. You can't go back there now. What would you do? You know they won't accept you there. There's nothing for you in Charleston anymore. Not even your teaching position. At least, Abigail, if you go with the party, you'll have something waiting for you when you get to Stone Valley."

Abigail began to cry.

Giving her his brightest smile, he said encouragingly, "When I get out of prison, I'll come join you," he promised.

Cabot looked at Gabe. He never really cared much for him. The man wasn't his class of people, the class he wanted for Abigail, but at least he knew that Gabe cared for Abigail and believed he could trust him to look out for her.

"Watch over her, Gabe. She's never been alone."

He handed his rifle and pistol to Gabe.

As sober-faced as he had ever been, Gabe took them and answered, "I'll do that, Newgate. You can count on me."

Abigail flew off of her horse and clung to Cabot's leg. "Papa, take me with you, please," she begged. "You need someone with you at a time like this."

He bent over and kissed the top of her head. "Let go now, Abigail," he said calmly. "Please let go. I promise I'll come join you someday." He pried her hands from his leg and, turning his horse toward the return journey, he straightened his back, bracing himself against her tears, and said to Sweeney, "Let's go."

As her father rode off, Abigail put her head in her hands and cried. Gabe stepped off his horse and put his arms around her. She laid her head against his chest, still sobbing. He would never have made such a bold move, but the intensity of the moment caused him to throw off all restraint.

Abigail cried silently all morning. When they stopped at mid-morning, she had little to say as she and Gabe took out provisions to eat.

Gabe cleared his throat. He was always at a loss as how to deal with women when they cried.

"Abigail." Never had he addressed her by her first name and he didn't notice the slip now. "If you want to talk about it, I'm here to listen."

She looked at him morosely. "What's there to say, Gabe? My father came from a good, upstanding family, pillars of the community, and now I find he's nothing but a common thief. He's ruined his family's good name. And most of all, I thought he was a Christian."

He cleared his throat again. "Don't judge him too harshly, Abigail. After all, man is not perfect and can fall from grace. A man will do desperate things and act in unusual ways sometimes when he's backed into a corner." He was silent for a moment. "I'm sure God forgives him, so perhaps you can find it in your heart to forgive him, too."

She stared at him incredulously. Gabe who avoided any talk of religion, is lecturing her on the grace of God?

He smiled sheepishly. "I'm not totally ignorant as to the ways of God. I know more than you realize."

"Apparently," she remarked, as she picked at her food.

"Eat," he admonished. "You need to keep your strength up. We've got some hard mountain travel just ahead."

"What's the point in going on?" she moaned. "I've lost everything."

"You've got everything to live for. You've got your position in Stone Valley waiting for you." He wanted to say "You've got me," but knew this wasn't the right time.

"Huh! If Jacob Templeton has found out about Father, he'll probably turn me out of the caravan," she spat contemptuously.

"You're wrong about the Reverend," Gabe defended. "He's just about the finest man I've ever met."

"I never thought my life would come to this," she lamented. "I'd always been so comfortable in Charleston with friends. There was music and books and...." Her thoughts trailed off as she thought of her old beau.

Gabe watched her intently. She couldn't fool him. He knew there had been someone else, knew it all along. He was waiting for her to close the door on her past and he was in no hurry.

CHAPTER THIRTY-ONE

IT WAS A STEEP CLIMB over formidable-looking Powell Mountain through Kane's Gap and a four-mile trek straight down the other side.

The view at the top was spectacular. Starting down the other side toward Powell Valley, the party dismounted their horses to make the precipitous climb down the mountain.

They were nearly down to the valley, just a half-mile away, when Ransom's packhorse stumbled and its load pitched forward. Ransom was caught off-balance and losing his foothold, went tumbling down the mountain. Landing on a protruding ledge, he was knocked unconscious.

Rachel cried out and inched down after him. The party came to a halt and the men, instantly alert, released their horses, grabbed their rifles, and began to move stealthily in the direction of Rachel's voice.

Will emerged from the crowd that was gathering, with Sam and James in tow.

"James! Go tell Father, Ransom is hurt and get Doc Stone!" shouted Will. "Hurry!"

Ransom had landed on his back, but his body was lying at an odd angle and blood began pooling at the back of his head.

As if from a dark distance, Ransom heard Rachel calling his name. "What's wrong now?" he thought. "Is she in trouble? I've got to get to her."

Swimming back to consciousness, his body, from the waist down, was numb, yet his brain was alive and clear.

I'm dying. I know it. Then this was how it felt to die.

He stared at Rachel leaning over him. His hazel eyes, that usually had a twinkling dance to them, were dilated enormously.

Ransom reached his hand to her and she took it, her eyes dull with shock.

"This was my dream," he uttered to her.

Rachel thought hard to all their talks during the nights.

Dream? What's he talking about? I don't remember any dream.

"Don't talk, Ransom," Will said. "Save your strength. Doc is coming."

Ransom shuddered. "I'm not going to make it, Will."

"Don't say that, Ransom!" Will argued heatedly. "You will make it! Stay strong!"

"Sam," Ransom gasped. "Where's Sam?"

"I'm here, Ransom," Sam said, as he knelt beside Ransom, his knuckles turning white as he gripped the edge of the ledge.

Releasing Rachel's hand to reach toward Sam and grasping his shirt, "Take care—take care of Rachel. Promise me!" he demanded. "Promise me, Sam!"

"Yes, yes," Sam answered. "You've got my word, Ransom. I promise, I'll take care of her."

He had never believed any premonition that Ransom had, not for a single moment. And it appeared all that Ransom had spoken of was now coming to pass. Why hadn't he taken him seriously?

Lying there with his lifeblood staining the ledge beneath him, Ransom looked again at Rachel. He lifted his arm as though to touch her, but fell back limp.

Straining with effort, he said, "Remember. Remember, all my love, always." His eyes glazed over and then closed, like a curtain shutting out the light.

Ransom was gone.

"This isn't real," Rachel thought. In spite of the hot day, cold prickled her skin. Cold that started inside, freezing her hands and feet. "It can't be. Not Ransom, who I love. Not the man who has been my mainstay in all that I've gone through."

Ransom the minister!

Ransom the missionary!

Ransom…her husband, who had shared his deepest thoughts and plans with her!

Gone! His life snuffed out in one disastrous moment! No! This wasn't happening, not to Ransom.

Inside, the reaction was hitting her. She was sick, wanted to get off alone, and she got off the ledge and dropped by the nearest tree. Her mind began to scream and scream, but no sound came out.

John appeared from the valley and summing up the situation, went to Rachel sitting white-faced.

Jacob and Elizabeth arrived in time to see Will scoop up some leaves and throw them into the air with a wrenching cry, "Nooo…."

Rachel began to scream again in her mind, and John lifted her up and carried her away. She tried to fight him, but he held her tight. Setting her down on his lap a few feet up the grade, he rocked her as she clawed at his arms, desperately trying to escape his unyielding grip. Away…she had to get away.

"I feel the life has gone out of me, Jacob," Elizabeth wept that night.

He pulled her closer into the crook of his arm.

"I think this whole journey is cursed," she said. "You know, I've always felt something was wrong about it. With Robert and Cordelia murdered, Mr. Newgate taken back to South Carolina, and now," she sobbed, "our Ransom is dead."

Jacob couldn't tell her the same voice of doubt had invaded his mind. Never had he known such sorrow before. He thought back to the funeral of Robert and Cordelia, and the many others he had officiated over the years, and the fact that he had never been able to fully identify with the mourners. He was sympathetic and tried his best to alleviate their suffering, but never could truly empathize.

He understood, all too well now. That unexplainable feeling, like an arm had been severed from your body, a part of you gone, that you could never get back. Something previously untouched and now broken, cut off, gone in a moment of time, never to be retrieved, and the feeling of grasping in thin air for answers.

No, he had no answer for this, but he knew in his heart that somehow God had not failed him. How could he curse God? Someone in the Bible was asked to do that very thing. Oh, yes. Job's wife. "Curse God and die," she had said.

But God was still faithful. This knowledge did not ease the pain of mourning, but God understood their pain, he was sure of that. He was grateful for the few short years that he had Ransom. Their relationship had been special. Ransom's uniqueness filled his mind as it skipped rapidly from one event of his childhood, and growing up, to another. His patience, godliness, and excellent spirit were always prominent in his young life.

His mind eventually turned to thoughts of Rachel. Ransom's last words were to her. What would become of her now? She was in absolute shock, unable to communicate her grief.

His heart was so heavy and anger began to bubble up within him. He was only a man, not God. Self-doubt riddled his thoughts. He was drowning and there was no one to offer him a lifeline. So often he had tried to help others in their suffering. He'd always been there in their troubles, offering encouragement.

But who would comfort him now? How much could he bear? Everyone expected him to be strong in spite of his own sorrow. But he was not strong, only human, and for a few terrifying, intense moments, he thought he would lose his mind. He wanted desperately to shake loose from Elizabeth and run, somewhere, anywhere to escape.

And I said, Oh that I had wings like a dove! For then would I fly away, and be at rest. Psalm 55:6

As the hours passed, acceptance of the day's events settled over him. *The Lord giveth and the Lord taketh away.* Words easily spoken in the past. Yet in spite of his own sorrow, he was still responsible for the souls of the people. He felt like Saint Paul. In writing to the Corinthian Church, that he sometimes despaired of life. Yes…for him, this was one of those times.

In the midst of confusion, one thing was certain. With a deep shudder, he was determined by the grace of God, that he would preside at his son's funeral. In the morning the funeral would take place, but not tonight. Jacob needed this night before he committed Ransom's body, once and for all, to the earth.

Jacob chose as his text Isaiah 40:31: *But they that wait upon the Lord shall renew their strength; they shall mount up with wings as eagles; they shall run, and not be weary; and they shall walk, and not faint.*

With tears streaming down his face, the Reverend talked of the goodness of God, and the blessing of knowing those that God had given to us in our short lives. Often raising his hands in praise unto God, he blessed the Lord.

Gabe stood on the outskirts of the gathering, hat in hand, as the other men gathered there. He had never liked funerals. Even more so, since the death of his wife and son, and he wouldn't have had one then, except his neighbors insisted. Funerals reminded him of eternity on the other side and that was something he hadn't been ready to come to grips with.

As Jacob preached, Gabe watched him earnestly. Jacob did not realize the impact his words were having on Gabe. Gabe's heart was melting from its iciness and tears began to fall unheeded down his face. This large, broad-shouldered man, whose hardness of heart intimidated most, broke…completely. Every harsh memory took on a sinuous quality in the river of life that was flowing.

When Jacob was concluding the service, Gabe turned to wait under a tree to one side. He felt sorry for the Templeton family, but wanted—no—not wanted—needed to talk to Jacob.

"Pardon me, Reverend," he said, as Jacob passed by, not waiting to see his son committed to the ground. "If you don't mind, I'd like to give my heart to the Lord right now. I see how the Lord is comforting you and I want that same relationship with him."

Jacob was humbled and fresh tears flowed. If there was any good thing to come from Ransom's death, it was that a sinner found his way to God. Throwing his arm around Gabe, Jacob prayed with him and Gabe received the Lord Jesus into his heart.

When the last clods of dirt had been thrown onto the grave, the soil was packed down hard and stones piled on top to protect Ransom's body from ravenous beasts.

John hurriedly gave the command to leave. He was concerned for Rachel. She had stood stone-faced and insensate by the grave and didn't cry. Thinking back to how he had behaved after his wife's death, how he withdrew emotionally for months, he worried that she, too, might have the same reaction.

Rachel never heard the sermon. Jacob could have been talking about the moon, for any sense of mind she had, for the words Jacob said had no meaning. They fell on unhearing ears—ears that could make no logic of anything. Eyes dry, as unshed tears dammed up in her heart.

Sam was opening the clappers on his cattle when John approached him.

"Sam, I'm moving Rachel to the front of the line so I can keep an eye on her. I want you to move to the front of the line, also, and stay close to her. Watch over her," John asked anxiously. "She has this tendency to run away when faced with unpleasant situations and I need you with her at all times."

John needn't have worried. Rachel was numb and unfeeling. Cold, like the iciness of a frozen river, lay over her emotions. It was difficult to remember to put one foot in front of the other, much less run away. John and Sam loaded her packhorses that morning. She refused to eat and had nothing to say.

"I know you have a lot on your hands with your own herds and packhorses, Sam. If you could lend a hand with Rachel's cattle, I'll relieve you of most guard duty and try my best to help all I can."

Sam nodded. "You can count on me, John," he answered, searching across the animals for a glimpse of her.

It wouldn't be easy keeping his word to Ransom and Sam wondered how in the world he would fulfill it. Oh, he could handle the finances all right. That was no problem. But, Rachel despised him, and it was his fault…only his fault. He had kept her at arm's length because she was Ransom's wife and he'd felt attracted to her. Too many times, he had seen bewilderment in her eyes. And he was wise enough in the world to know that she was mystified by his behavior, thinking there was some fault in her.

"At least the going will be easier for the next twenty-five miles through this valley," John noted with a sigh of relief, cutting through Sam's thoughts. "The trail follows the creek bottoms and crisscrosses back and forth across the waterways. It's level and will become broader and more open as we travel on."

CHAPTER THIRTY-TWO

THEY TRAVELED THROUGH THE VALLEY along the Powell River until the shadows of the trees grew long. The funeral had given them a late start, so they had only come about eight miles today. The sun was setting and they camped for the night.

Sam had searched his mind all day for words to comfort Rachel, but the look on her face defied intrusion into her bruised thoughts. He doubted that she realized he was there, anyway, as sitting astride her horse, she slumped in the saddle and blindly followed the lead of John and Sam. Yesterday's tragedy had drained her of all feeling. When they stopped for their mid-day meal, Rachel forced herself to look her father in the eyes, but turned her head away from the food he offered.

John was distressed. No one could reach her and he was at a loss what to do. If she would only cry or display some feeling, she could be comforted. This apparent lack of emotion was driving him to distraction and he felt he was walking on eggshells.

As Sam and John took care of the herds, Cissa brought food to the front of the line.

"Here, honey, I've brought you something to eat." Cissa felt bad. She'd seen the state that Rachel was in and she should have been there by her side today. Torn between staying with James and his family, in their own sorrow, and Rachel, she had worried all day and was relieved when John finally announced they were stopping to camp.

For the first time that day, Rachel spoke. Shaking her head, she said dully, "I don't think I can eat, Cissa."

"Just try a little." She tore the ham and what was the last of the cheese into small pieces.

"Put some in your mouth and see if you can eat."

Cissa kept insisting, until at last, Rachel ate a little.

"That's better," Cissa noted with satisfaction.

"Oh, Cissa!" Rachel finally whispered as she clutched Cissa's arm frantically. "I keep thinking about Ransom and how he's so alone back there. How can I go off and leave him out in this wilderness?"

"Well, dearest, you have no other choice," Cissa informed her as she handed her a cup of water.

Dislodging her hand from Cissa's arm and wrapping her hands around the cup and taking a sip, Rachel declared, "I'll never get over this."

"I don't think anyone expects you to," she agreed.

"We had so many plans," Rachel fretfully informed her.

"I know you did," coaxing her to drink again.

Rachel took another sip and said, "He wanted to build us a fine home and have lots of children."

"I know he did," taking the cup and giving her a pewter plate of food. "He was a good man."

Cissa took a piece of ham from the plate and made her eat it.

Rachel swallowed the ham and said, "And most of all...he wanted to be a missionary."

Cissa thought about that for a moment.

"I guess the missionary part came true in a way."

Rachel looked at her. "What do you mean?"

"Gabe gave his heart to the Lord today at the funeral."

Rachel stared at Cissa, trying to comprehend what she said. "Gabe prayed?"

That was unbelievable. He was the most disrespectful and hardened individual she had ever met. Of all the people she knew, Gabe was the last person she expected to pray.

"Yes," Cissa said, a slight smile touching the corners of her mouth. "Don't you remember?"

"No." Rachel shook her head. "I don't remember anything about the funeral."

"Well, he did," Cissa confirmed. "You might say that Gabe was a soul that Ransom won to God."

Rachel was dumfounded. She vaguely heard the soulful babbling, but the words never penetrated her grief. Except for her, Ransom had never mentioned winning any other souls to Christ, but she knew that was his heart's desire. At least something good had come out of this heart-breaking situation.

Cissa rose to her feet. "I think you'll feel a little better if you take a bath at the creek. How about it?" she cajoled. "Want to join me?"

Rachel finally nodded and Cissa said, "Good. Finish your food and drink your water and I'll get my things and come back for you."

After bathing, as Cissa combed her hair, Rachel closed her eyes and relaxed back against her, remembering her mother's gentle touch. She missed Mother and still thought of her every day. If there was any comfort at all, it was the knowledge that Ransom was with her now.

"You have such beautiful black hair, Rachel," Cissa remarked.

"I could just braid some strands on both sides and tie them up. Let's try that. And I'll put a ribbon in your hair."

John and Sam returned as Cissa was finishing tying the scarlet ribbon in Rachel's hair. "Jane has food for you men if you'll go get it," she instructed.

As John walked by Cissa, he silently mouthed the words, "Thank you."

∞∞∞∞∞∞∞∞∞∞∞∞∞∞∞∞∞

Rachel slept very little that night. Her mind continually replayed the accident and everything Cissa had told her. When she closed her eyes, the memory of Ransom tumbling down the mountainside, and how he looked just before he passed away, tormented her, causing her to flip from side to side in an effort to escape the memory.

And in the midst of the terrifying visions, Ransom's last request replayed again and again in her mind. Why would Ransom ask Sam to take care of her? Sam of all people! They didn't get along, Ransom knew that. Of all people to be obliged to, surely not Sam Spencer!

And now Sam had bound himself to her with a promise to Ransom! To think that Sam would be a part of her life now! He knew too much about her, she was sure of it, especially her divorce, and she was uncomfortable in his presence. With her dislike of him so strong, and his contempt for her, it was unthinkable that they would be bound together by a death promise.

She would just have to think of a way to release Sam from that vow!

Why not Pa? Why didn't Ransom ask him? She couldn't understand the reasoning of it all. She was glad Gabe became a Christian and that, at least, part of Ransom's dreams had been fulfilled.

"Oh, Ransom, Ransom. What shall I do? What's wrong with me? Why does everyone leave me?" she asked into the air.

She felt sick with regret as she thought of Ransom lying in the hastily dug grave. He was so alone back there in his mound of earth and stone while she still had people all around her trying to comfort her. "We just took off and left him. Somehow, that doesn't seem right."

Suddenly, it occurred to her that she'd never told Ransom goodbye. How could she go any farther on this journey? Unfinished business, she thought. Always running away from something in the past, she needed to make her peace with him, let him know that she could not stay. She'd been too numb to tell him goodbye before and it was imperative that she bid him farewell.

CHAPTER THIRTY-THREE

A LIGHT, THAT WAS NOT FULL LIGHT, gave promise the sun would soon be rising.

Rachel had not undressed the night before, and climbing quietly from her tent, Rachel smoothed out her skirt as much as possible, put on her moccasins, and started back for Ransom's grave.

Thick, gray fog hung heavily in the air, draping the valley like a shroud. Like the dew that lingered on the blades of grass, the damp, murky mist clung to her hair and clothing.

Sam came awake with a start, not knowing what he heard.

What now? he thought, attempting to get up. One foot was asleep, and he moved it until feeling came back again. Pulling on his boots and climbing from his tent, he looked about him.

All was quiet. The fire was dying with the snap of the remaining coals. Could that have been what he had heard? He didn't think so. Could it possibly be an animal? He listened, but there was no noise.

There was no sound from Rachel's tent, and crossing to it, he then saw she was gone.

Thinking she had gone to relieve herself, he waited a few minutes and when she didn't return, he retrieved his hat and proceeded to investigate the camp.

Barely had she passed unnoticed through the middle of the caravan, when Sam, as lithe as an Indian, caught noiselessly up with her.

Grasping her arm, "Where do you think you are going, Rachel?" he demanded in a hoarse whisper.

He startled her for all were asleep.

"I—I'm going back to Ransom's grave," she stammered as she pulled against his hold.

"You little fool!" his words were hard, but tempered with softness. "You can't do that. We'll be breaking camp soon and it's several miles back there."

Rachel looked away.

Finally: "You don't understand. I must."

Dropping her arm and tipping back his hat with his forefinger, "Suppose you tell me *why* you must?" he questioned, his hands on his hips.

"Because Ransom's so alone back there," she answered simply.

Her answer left him a little speechless. What did she intend to do? Camp out by his grave?

"That may be, but you can't just go running off by yourself. You haven't taken any provisions or a horse. Just how far did you think you were going to get?"

"I was afraid that someone would notice that I was leaving," she said uncertainly.

"That's what the guards are there for, Rachel," he replied in an exasperated tone. "Don't you understand the danger in doing such a thing? You could be kidnapped or killed by Indians."

For the first time since Ransom's death, tears hovered on her eyelids, tears that threatened to slide down her cheeks. She looked up into his eyes with one quick beseeching glance, and in that look, was the agony of heartbreak.

"Sam, I—I never told Ransom goodbye," she confided, as her lids fluttered down again.

What to do? He could understand somewhat her need to do what she was asking, but it was a reckless thing to undertake, under the circumstances. She had a way about her that was breaking his resolve, and that he wasn't used to. Silently, for a few moments, he watched emotions flit across her face as the mist swirled around them, trying its best to break free from the earthen floor to dissipate into the sun's first morning rays.

"We'll go talk to John about it first," Sam said, finally relenting. "There's no point running off. He'll worry about you if we don't tell him and the whole camp will be in an uproar."

Frowning at his suggestion, Rachel was certain that her father would not let her go. He had enough on his shoulders looking after the party, and, now her, since Ransom's death and would refuse to be hampered with worry about her leaving to go back. When John Winslow made up his mind about something, there was no changing it.

Oh! If only she had been more quiet upon leaving this morning! She could have been well on her way. "Still," she mused, "they would have come looking for me, and that would have been worse." She loved her pa, but when he gave an order, he expected it to be obeyed. "Perhaps," she thought, "if I could persuade Sam to go with me."

Their eyes met. Hers—naked with pleading, his—cool as the chipped ice from the springhouse that was served in cider in summer.

"Can't we—can't you and I just—"

"No!" Sam uttered, a nerve fluttering in his cheek. He cleared his throat and unconsciously leaned back, farther away from her. Those dark eyes were appealing and he refused to allow himself to fall under their spell. He longed to hold her and comfort her, but he didn't dare. He turned abruptly on his heel to walk back and she followed reluctantly, fearing that her father would, without a doubt, go against her wishes.

The sun was breaking through the foggy curtain as they walked back into the front of the camp. She stood anxiously by her tent while Sam talked to John.

"I know it's a foolhardy thing to do, John, but unless she does this, it will be hard for her to move on emotionally."

John heaved a big sigh.

"It's against my better judgment," he said finally, "but if you can round up enough men to go with you, we'll meet you at the crossing of the Powell River."

Glancing at Rachel, he added, "Take care of her, Sam. She's my only child."

"I know, John," Sam said. "You can count on me."

They rode at a moderate pace, scanning the valley floor, keeping an eye out for Indians, until finally they reached the end of the valley at mid-morning.

Overhead, a buzzard wheeled in long, lazy circles, and for a minute Sam thought the grave had been spoiled.

But, no, he saw the stones were undisturbed.

As James and Tom picketed the horses on the thick grass, Tom looked across the saddle at Rachel, sitting astride her horse, staring at Ransom's grave. It had been difficult for him to offer condolences to her as he was still gripped in the throes of his brother's death, and he silently struggled with his own thoughts about the worth of the journey.

Finally: stepping down from her horse, Rachel started to walk toward the grave. Her legs began to shake and nearly buckled. Sam took her arm.

Pulling against his grip, she fell down across the mound of rocks.

She had lost her best friend. He'd left her alone in a mad and desolate world. Memories flooded her mind, taking her back to Wellington. It all came back to her, her mother dying and her father departing for Kentucky, leaving her behind. Ransom had taken her under his wing.

She thought back to times past, such as, when she was raped two years ago in Wellington by Wade Bennett. Ransom showed up and nearly killed Wade. When she insisted on wearing britches at the mill, Ransom took up for her against the talk of the town. He was there when she was in labor and delivered her premature baby and then presided over its funeral.

When Peter divorced her, Ransom married her, despite the disapproval of others, without waiting for a word of love from her. He had kept a continual watch over her, shielding her from life's uncertainties and difficulties.

She had come to love him and his goodness. How could she let him go? Who would she confide in now? Who would guide her in the affairs of life like Ransom had?

As the men kept watch, slowly, at first, then in successive bouts, she released healing tears.

She lay weeping a long time.

As she lay across his grave, she sensed Ransom speaking to her. *Go on. Fulfill the dreams we had. Don't stop now. Spread your wings and fly.* And from the past came the echoing voice of her mother, *God won't put on you more than you can bear.*

She had existed on the dreams and wishes of others her whole life, but now, with a mounting certainty, she realized she was being released to walk in her own destiny, to fulfill God's plan for her own life.

Finally, she struggled to her feet. As an afterthought, she reached up, and from her entwined, black strands, worked loose the ribbon that Cissa had fixed in her hair the night before. Crouching down, she tied it around the crude, hastily fashioned cross.

"I'll have to see to it that Ransom has a decent stone placed on his grave, so those that pass this way will know that here lies a good man," she promised herself.

Like a fire that has been doused by a departing camper, its smoking ashes reminiscent of the once warming, blazing fire, Rachel said her final, soft goodbye to Ransom's remains, and rose resolutely to begin living life once again.

Straightening her back, pushing back her loosened hair, and wiping the dirt and tears from her face, she turned from the grave and walked to her horse that dozed in the trees.

Mounting, and looking straight ahead, she said, "I'm ready now."

It was evening when they arrived back at camp. The party was waiting for them at Powell River.

"We'll cross in the morning," John informed them.

He peered at Rachel and then at Sam. Sam nodded to him that everything was all right. John let out an almost imperceptible small breath. For the first time in the last week, it seemed like the beginning of a good night.

CHAPTER THIRTY-FOUR

THE NEXT MORNING SAM was about to throw Rachel's saddle over her horse when a resounding "No!" stopped him.

"I've decided to ride Ransom's sorrel," Rachel announced with a note of authority in her voice, a turned-up chin, and determined look on her face.

She didn't like Sam, no matter what promise Ransom had made him make. And no matter that her father had delegated him to keep watch over her. She was the head of the family now, such as it was.

He shrugged. "I've got to saddle your horse anyway. Can't leave the saddle behind."

He stood back and watched as she doggedly walked to the sorrel, practically dragging Ransom's saddle with her, and with great effort, finally heaved the saddle over the animal as it turned its head to look at her, and swished its tail.

She turned to give Sam a look that triumphantly said, "I told you so."

As he wrinkled his brow and ran his finger across the bridge of his nose, it was clear to him what was going through her mind.

Turning back to saddle her horse, Sam wasn't fooled. She was in charge now…or at least thought she was. She would squall like a mashed cat when she found out about Ransom's will, and that was not an event he was looking forward to. To find out that Ransom had willed that Sam preside over Rachel's affairs until she turned twenty-five, would unsettle her to no end.

"Better have John present when I read Rachel the will," Sam thought, and he intended to put that off until they took possession of the Stone Valley land.

Sam had been hovering over Rachel all morning and it was getting on her nerves.

"Honestly! You'd think from the way he acts that I can't take care of myself!" She didn't mind when Pa offered help, but something about Sam rubbed her the wrong way.

He knew she was irritated with him, but he just let it roll off as though he hadn't noticed a thing. He took her packhorses by their reins, but she jerked them out of his hand.

"All right, little girl," Sam said as one side of his mouth turned up. "Have it your way."

Being the head of the party, John and Rachel crossed Powell River first. Not realizing how deep the river was, she prodded her horse ahead, pulling the packhorses along. Her horse began to swim and with a sudden jolt of the reins, she was jerked back, loosening her hold on the reins of the packhorses. She fell into the water with a startled cry.

Sam stood on the bank and chuckled at her dilemma. Then taking off his boots, he swam out to get her. When Rachel felt Sam grab hold of her, she gasped, "Take your hands off me, you fool. I can swim."

He ignored her seething words and brought her to shore on the other side.

Standing up, she shook off his arms in a rage and ran her hands over her wet hair. "You—you!" she didn't know any names to call him. "I told you I could swim! You almost made me drown," she sputtered.

"That may be," Sam smirked, pointing to the river, "but you've lost some of your load in the water. See if you can salvage what's still floating before it sinks to the bottom," he countered and walked back into the water to swim back to the other side to bring his own horses and the livestock across.

Rachel swung around and glared at the clothes that were floating on the water. Stomping her foot, she cried, "Pa!"

Sitting astride his horse, he looked at her and threw up his hands. "You're on your own, Rachel. If you're determined not to accept any help from Sam, then I'll let you know right now, that your stubbornness will get you nowhere." Putting his hands on the pommel, he nonchalantly remarked, "Better hurry if you're going to get those clothes!"

Sam stood on the other side amused as she stormed into the water and retrieved her clothes. His eyes twinkled as he watched her wring the water from her belongings, fretting all the while.

"I've never met such a stubborn woman in all my life!" he thought as he gave his head a little shake.

∞∞∞∞∞∞∞∞∞∞∞∞∞∞∞∞

Gabe Roswell had moved his tent next to Abigail's to watch over her.

There was a definite change in him since he became a Christian, Abigail readily acknowledged. Where he had been obtuse and insensitive, he was now thoughtful and kind. And he'd given up that awful habit of tobacco. That, in itself, was a major feat. She let her guard down and actually enjoyed the time they spent together. She'd never had a man to look after her other than her father. It was obvious, to her delight, he entertained feelings for her, and she basked in his attention. True, he never spoke words of love to her, but his gray eyes looked at her with yearning.

He had intended to wait until they reached Stone Valley to propose to her. But never one to waste any time, he decided to ask Abigail to marry him as they sat in front of the fire one night after supper.

"Miss Abigail?" he asked as he cleared his throat.

Abigail looked at Gabe and was surprised to see a nervous look on his face.

"Yes, Gabe?" she arched her eyebrows.

"It could not have escaped you by now that I…uh…we seem to be fairly well matched."

Fairly well matched? She was silent. They didn't have much in common from what she could see except now he had become a Christian. She was educated, he wasn't. She liked books and art and guessed that he didn't. He was an outdoorsman. She wasn't. He was outgoing and assertive. She was introverted and quiet.

Gabe continued, "And since our circumstances don't lend to a long engagement, I would be honored if you would become my wife."

She pressed her lips together. She would have liked a little romance to be included in his proposal of marriage.

"Hmm," she uttered thoughtfully. Putting her finger to her cheek, she finally asked, "Let me see if I understand you correctly. You're asking me to marry you, am I right, Mr. Roswell?"

He nodded his head yes and thought, "Uh, oh. She's calling me by my last name again."

"And what my father has done doesn't have any bearing upon your decision? That he's now known openly as a thief?"

He shrugged. "Why should it? It's you I'm asking, not him."

Having never received a proposal of marriage before, she was enjoying the moment and wanted to savor every second.

"Well, you do have one thing going for you. You've become a Christian." He hadn't mentioned love and after all of her novel reading, she desperately wanted someone to unabashedly declare love for her, such as Phillip had. She would never forget Phillip, not for her whole lifetime, she knew this as surely as the sun rose and set.

Gazing closely at Gabe, she examined his face—every line, the way his eyes crinkled at the corners, his full lips, and watchful gray eyes. She wondered if she could learn to love him as she still loved Phillip. Phillip had known the things to do, the words to say, to make her feel special in a city that had cast her off as second-hand goods.

Even if she missed her only chance for marriage, she refused to settle for a marriage that was less than romantic. This had been her long-standing dream, and if it meant spinsterhood for the rest of her life, she would not compromise. Not now. Not ever.

"I'll have to think it over, Mr. Roswell," Abigail said decidedly.

He blinked hard and nearly sputtered. He thought she would readily agree. What was she holding out for? He'd been so solicitous and kind toward her and they were getting on so well that he thought by now she would be ready to accept.

Well, he would find out what her reservation was. That was for certain.

THIRTY-FIVE

JOHN AND SAM were hobbling the horses and opening the bells on the cattle while Rachel unpacked and prepared the evening meal.

"Sam, I want to apologize for Rachel's behavior these last few days," John said.

"Forget it, John," he said easily.

"I've tried to talk to her, but she totally ignores what I have to say about it." John ran his hand over his jaw, looking as weary as he sounded. "She acts like she's her own boss now."

John stopped suddenly. "But there is something I can do for you."

At the question in Sam's eyes, John said, "Send Will up here. He can trade places with you for a couple of days. Dealing with Ransom's oldest brother, maybe Rachel will calm down a little."

"All right," he said, "I'll do that. But there's something that I've been meaning to bring up to you, John," Sam ventured. "Ransom had a feeling something was going to happen to him before he died."

"Is that so?" John questioned over a cow's head.

"Yes. And what Rachel doesn't know is that Ransom made a will," Sam confessed. Pointing to camp where his provisions were, "It's in my saddlebag." He paused and frowned. "John…she's not going to like what's in the will."

"How's that?" John asked, darting a practiced eye over the camp doings.

Sam's frown deepened as he said, "He made me executor and trustee over her financial affairs until she's twenty-five."

John was taken aback. "Whew! That's gonna make the pot blow its top!"

"Exactly," a dark shadow crossed Sam's face. "I as much as said so to Ransom."

"What'd he say to that?" he wanted to know.

Sam looked John straight in the eye. "That I could handle it."

Something flickered behind John's eyes and he was silent for a while.

"Then you know that I'm holding her money for her," John finally offered.

"Yes. Ransom told me." Sam felt a little awkward that it was he, and not John, who was in charge of Rachel's affairs. "I want you to take care of it, though, until we get to Stone Valley. I'll draw up the papers necessary to transfer the funds to me."

Sam's shoulders stooped ever so slightly as though the burden had already shifted to him. "I've got to figure how to get her spread producing, as well as mine."

"Strange," John thought, "that Ransom should pick Sam to be executor of his will. The contention is so strong between Rachel and Sam." John laughed to himself. "Sparks flying between a man and woman, doesn't always mean hate, although in this case, it sure comes pretty close."

All the same, with the trips he would be making back to Virginia, John realized that he wouldn't be around for Rachel much at times. That could have been the reason for Ransom's choice. Still, a small dart of hurt entered him to know that he had been passed over as Rachel's protector. He still smarted with guilt when he thought back to the time that he had deposited Rachel on the Reverend's doorstep after his wife died. He had let her down when she needed him the most. Those were the kinds of things a person didn't easily forget. Thank goodness, Rachel never threw it in his face. "Guess Ransom made the right choice after all, in choosing Sam," he thought regretfully.

"Well, Sam, I can be there for a while," said John. "I'll help Frank raise a cabin for her and I'll try to help her some on her place, but I've got to take care of mine also. And fall of next year, I'll be driving the herds back East to sell. And any others back East who want to come to Green River Country, I'll lead back."

"He told me that too. That was pretty much his reason for his decision."

Sam added, "There's something you need to know. He did choose you as alternate executor."

That relieved John somewhat. "Another thing, John," Sam paused while laying his hand on a cow's back. "I'm asking you to be there when I read her the will."

John glanced up briefly as he hobbled a horse, "You've got a peck of trouble on your hands, Sam. She's my daughter, but she's got a temper, too. Too independent and self-reliant. Never took much after her mother, except in looks. Her mother was one of the sweetest women there ever was. I guess Rachel spent too much time with me when she was growing up." He bent to hobble another horse. "There's good I can say about her, though. She's honest and straightforward—not a deceitful bone in her body. And she gives everything of herself to help."

Something you neglected to mention, thought Sam as he removed his hat and rumpled his red hair. *She's incredibly beautiful and when I look into her eyes, I can see straight into her heart.*

∞∞∞∞∞∞∞∞∞∞∞∞∞∞∞

That evening, Gabe stopped by the Templeton section of the camp. The men were tending to the livestock and he hoped that he might slip in unobserved by the ladies. Cissa and Jane gave him a cursory glance, but they were engrossed in the business of making camp and paid him little attention.

Elizabeth had gathered wood and was in the process of building a fire.

Careful that no one overhear, Gabe whispered, "Mrs. Templeton?"

He startled her. She looked up and whispered back. "What is it, Mr. Roswell?"

"Ma'am, I don't mean to disturb you."

With a wave of her hand, she dismissed his statement.

"I need to speak to you…in private."

Looking around, she spotted an empty bucket and handed it to him. "We can walk to the creek and talk on the way."

Out of earshot of the others, Elizabeth asked, "What is so confidential that you needed to speak to me, Mr. Roswell?"

"Ma'am…I've got a problem."

Immediately she was all ears. "You have? What's your problem, Mr. Roswell?"

"Umm…I've asked Miss Abigail to marry me and for some reason she's putting me off."

"Did you ask her why, Mr. Roswell?" she interrogated.

"No, ma'am." He shook his head. "I didn't want to push it too far."

She was silent for a moment as he waited in anticipation.

She'd noticed the relationship blossoming between them and though she was initially against the match, she now conceded, in light of the fact that he had become a Christian, that perhaps it might be the plan of God.

"Just what do you want *me* to do about it?"

He shuffled his feet as he lowered his head. "Would you talk to her, ma'am, and find out what's holding up her decision?"

She hesitated. "I don't know, Mr. Roswell. Abigail and I are not that close. That's kind of snooping into personal affairs." The instant she said it, she laughed as she realized that had never stood in her way before.

Drumming her fingers against her skirt, she questioned, "Let me ask you this, Mr. Roswell. Have you courted her properly?"

"What do you mean, ma'am?"

"You know. Brought her some flowers…told her how pretty she is…things like that. And let me ask you something personal. Do you love her?" she asked candidly.

"Oh, yes, ma'am," he answered with a beaming smile on his face. "With all my heart!"

"Did you tell *her* that?" Elizabeth asked.

He tipped back his hat and rubbed his head. "To be perfectly honest, I didn't do any of those things. I just figured once I proposed, she'd accept."

"Mr. Roswell, knowing women as I do, I'd say therein lies your problem," said Elizabeth vigorously. "You must tell her things like…how pretty her eyes are and that you've been waiting for a girl just like her. A woman loves to hear words like that and treasures them."

He gave her a smile so pleasant and grateful that Elizabeth stood uncertainly for a moment. She hated to admit that she had misjudged the man. Daring to pursue the subject further, she decided to broach him about Abigail's feelings. "May I ask you something else?" continued Elizabeth. "Does she love you?"

He looked her in the eyes with all sincerity.

"I think she does, ma'am. Yes, even if she doesn't admit it, I *know* she does."

CHAPTER THIRTY-SIX

SAM HAD MOVED HIS CAMP TO THE FRONT AGAIN and for the next couple of days the westward-bound company followed the path that snaked higher and higher up into the hills. In this seemingly limitless forest, the trees stretched so tall they couldn't see the tops. Thick moss covered the ground and the giant roots of trees like a thick, green, winter blanket. The canopy of the trees blotted out the brightness of the sun.

From far away, there was a droning noise, as though a swarm of bees had left their hive and was flying closer.

John raised his head and reined his horse to stop. Raising in his saddle, "What is that strange sound?" he asked aloud.

It began to rain. Not the soft rain of a shower, but torrential rains that brought mighty winds howling through the trees and trying desperately to invade the mausoleum of forest.

The wind hit them hard, like a roof falling in. The forest that seemed so impenetrable was yielding to a force greater than its own. Branches exploded in all directions.

Those at the front of the party were swept off their horses. Tumbling down, they scrambled to hold life and limb together.

With no time to think, Sam knocked Rachel to the ground and covered her, using his body for protection. The twirling wind picked him up and slammed him into a massive tree, its roots, like tentacles, holding him as Rachel was also hurled into the air, landing eventually in a mass of underbrush that wrapped tightly around her. The screams of the party were lost in the roaring of the wind. As it turned and whirled, whipping branches and leaves and anything else it could suck up, trees were uprooted as though they were toothpicks.

Within a few seconds, as quickly as it had come, it abated. Cattle and horses had scattered and been swept away with what provisions had not been wrenched from the packsaddles.

"Great guns!" John declared. "Must have been some type of cyclone!"

Sam untangled himself from roots that had been stripped of their bark by the gale and stumbled to his feet.

"Rachel?" he called dazedly, trying to get his bearings. "Where are you, Rachel?"

The bawling of cattle, whinnies from horses, and the ruckus from the rest of the party filled his ears, but as he strained to hear Rachel's soft voice, there was only silence.

"My word!" Sam thought in horror. "Where is she?" Staggering forward, wiping fragments of leaves from his face, he called again and again, "Rachel!" Climbing over huge branches ripped violently from trees, he was nearly in a panic.

"Dear God!" he prayed, "don't let her be dead!"

Desperately scrambling through the forest, pushing aside dislodged branches and other wreckage as he went, he called and called for her. Finally, he saw her feet peeking out from the brush she was entangled in, one moccasin ripped from her foot.

Tearing the thorny brush apart, heedless of the briars slashing his flesh, he finally released her from the prickly prison she was in.

"Rachel! Rachel, please answer me!" he demanded, crouching down and lifting her head onto his arm, as his bleeding hand quickly searched her scratched face for signs of life.

She had a hard time getting a deep breath—it seemed as if the wind had sucked the air right out of her lungs! Her nostrils were filled with the dirt and leaves that settled down around them.

Shaken and exhausted, Rachel feebly slapped at Sam's hands until he laid her down again on the barbed cushion of underbrush.

Rachel lay there for a while, eyes closed, savoring the pleasure of God-given life, and as she breathed deeply, her shaking eventually came to a stop. Opening her eyes, she looked into Sam's own anxious ones. Noting his drenched, curly hair, she lifted a hand to her own and found it was wet, too.

"Are you all right, Rachel?" Sam asked as he helped her to sit.

There wasn't much that frightened her, but this incident had shaken her up considerably. Leaning over and drawing her weak forearm across her head, she answered in a strangled voice, "I think so."

He looked at his bleeding hands. He thought he had lost her. The depth of emotion that had driven him like a madman, clawing at the brush to rescue her, frightened him. Always calculating and cool-headed, it came as a complete surprise to him that he was capable of such intense feelings.

But he wasn't looking for a relationship with a woman. Not now, not with so much on his agenda. Fearing that he was becoming emotionally entangled, he desperately needed to get away from Rachel and let his emotions settle down.

"Good!" he said, rising swiftly to his feet. "I'm going to round up the animals."

She struggled to get up, "I'll go with you," she said, giving a cough.

"No!" he said, a little too quickly. "Better you stay put. You might get lost in this forest if you start traipsing around looking for the livestock." Giving her a swift once over, "I'll come back for you," he reassured her.

Rachel was up now and her brows drew into a frown. "Some of those cattle belong to me, too, Sam Spencer!" Crossing her arms and declaring in a voice that had not completely recovered, "I said, Mr. Spencer, I'm going with you!"

He almost laughed at her obstinacy in her bedraggled state. Her wet hair had been blown about wildly and bits of leaves and twigs clung to the tendrils.

"Suit yourself." He shrugged and walked away without waiting for her.

She followed after him and after a time, Rachel caught sight of Ransom's sorrel in the thick, mangled underbrush.

"There's Ransom horse!" Rachel cried as she began to climb over matted roots and through woody debris that had slammed against massive trees.

Something was wrong! Standing with his head dispiritedly low, he didn't look up at the sound of Rachel's voice.

Reaching him, she gave a desperate wail. "Oh, Sam, his leg is broken!" Stroking his mane, she whimpered, "Poor baby!"

Sam picked his way rapidly through the wreckage and reaching the horse, crouched to inspect his leg.

"I'm sorry, Rachel," Sam said contritely as he rose up. "He's got to be put down."

"No, Sam!" she said, clutching his arm. "Isn't there something you can do? Can't you save him?"

She couldn't let him go! Not Ransom's horse!

"Please!" Rachel beseeched.

He looked at her with pity. She'd had a bad time of it lately, with Ransom dying…and now this last vestige of life that belonged to Ransom…his horse. If there was anything in the world he could do to make it right, he would, but there wasn't, he mused ruefully.

Shaking his head, he told her softly, "You know there isn't, honey. It's got to be done." He paused and looked at her speculatively.

"It's better if you leave, Rachel," he advised. "Your father's calling you." He gave her a nudge. "Go."

She didn't know if she had the strength to walk away. She had missed Ransom acutely since his death and when riding his prized horse, she felt a part of him was still with her. Killing him would be the final stroke that would take Ransom from her life completely. She turned sideways from Sam and lifted her eyes toward the treetops, trying to hold back the tears.

She started to walk away, then, turning back toward the horse, Rachel laid her head on his neck.

Sam was right, she knew that. She'd been around animals enough to know that nothing else could be done. But she wouldn't walk away this time without saying goodbye.

Raising her head, Rachel looked the horse in the eye and rubbing his nose, forced herself to utter words past the huge lump in her throat. "Goodbye, old friend," she choked with a lingering kiss. "Ransom's waiting for you."

Turning to go, and with one last backward glance, Rachel yelled in a voice that suddenly cracked, "Here, Pa!"

John stopped as Rachel, with tears streaming down her face, picked her way through the rubble and walked up to him.

"What's wrong?" he asked, concerned. "Where's Sam? Is he hurt?"

"It's Ransom's horse, Pa," she replied grimly. "His leg is bro—
"

The report of a pistol rang out. With a gasp, she winced. Her shoulders sagging, she knew the sorrel was dead.

John and Rachel returned to the party in time to hear Will say to men gathered around him, "The storm only hit the front end of the party." Will gave a fleeting look at them. Everyone now but Sam had been found, and giving John a questioning look, he said instead, "If you men could help those in front to gather the herds back in...."

CHAPTER THIRTY-SEVEN

THEY HAD TRAVELED nearly one-hundred miles from the blockhouse and sixty miles before that.

The White Rocks, light-colored capstone of the Cumberlands, heralded the fact that they were approaching the hidden gap that would take them through the mountains. A few hours later they discovered the J-shaped dent whose gentle ascent, created by a long-vanished river, allowed them to pass over the divide and into Kentucky. The north wall of the gap was steep and rocky and much higher than the south side. In front of the party, Sam, John, and Will discussed moving ahead.

John's eyes nervously scouted the gap. "We need to move as quickly as possible. We've been on The Great Warriors' Path for a while."

Sam drew his brows together. "What's the Great Warriors' Path, John?"

"It's the main route between the Indian villages on Lake Erie and those to the south in Tennessee River country. We'd better not stay any longer than we have to. Likely as not, we could run into

Indians. Get the word out that we're moving on and tell the men to keep their eyes open."

They were met by a small party heading back towards Virginia, three men and two women. They had traveled from near Harrodsburg, their packhorses loaded with gear. A skinny, straggle- haired older woman had lost her husband and children to an Indian attack a long time ago and finally giving up after never finding another man to marry, decided to return to her kin in Virginia. The woman accompanying her had persuaded her husband to return also.

"Wasn't worth all the trouble," she said, as they had gone to Kentucky to get rich. Stories by Eastern writers had drawn them to the area, descriptive of riches and paradise. But with the land covered with trees and game growing scarce around Harrodsburg, they considered that the good life they had heard about just wasn't there.

Listening to their conversations, Jane looked anxiously for an opportunity to speak privately to the women, but they were in a hurry to press on. She nearly asked to return with them, but considering the dangers they had already come through, thought it best to stick with a large party such as theirs. Although as far as she was concerned, they were headed in the wrong direction.

Gabe thought over Elizabeth's suggestions thoroughly and after rehearsing words he would say to win over Abigail, decided to try some gallantry as Elizabeth had proposed. It wouldn't be long before they reached Stone Valley and as he had her to himself each evening, hoped this would be the night that she would say yes.

He'd kept his eyes open as they traveled, searching for wildflowers to present her with, but found none. He thought he'd seen some this afternoon, but to his disappointment it was merely the sun shining on a beech tree.

Supper was over, fried johnnycakes had been put aside for breakfast and lunch, and the three-legged skillet, iron pots, and dishes were washed.

After the dishwater had been dumped, Gabe sat down on the ground near Abigail and asked, "Abigail—Miss Newgate," he stumbled, "knowing you as I do, I know you've been giving a lot of thought to my proposal."

She opened her mouth to respond.

His heart began to race and cutting her off before a word passed over her lips, he said, "To be perfectly honest, I'm not the best-looking or best-educated man in the world, but I'll try my very best to make you happy. I've never wanted another woman after my wife died—that is, until you came along. You're beautiful and with all my heart, I'm asking you again to be my wife."

Abigail had enjoyed the flirtatious overtures that Gabe had been making the last few days. But she couldn't enter into a marriage with secrets about her background. Suddenly, she was fearful. If she told him all about her past, he might very well spurn her. She didn't know how he would react, but that was a chance she would just have to take. No more time for games. This was the telling moment.

Taking a slow breath, she said, "Gabe," moving slightly away from the fire, "let's take a walk."

Reaching the creek, here and there, she picked out familiar faces she had come to know and asked that they move out of earshot of anyone who might overhear. Reaching a fallen log, he offered his hand as she sat down.

After sitting in silence awhile, gathering her thoughts as to exactly what she would say, she began. "Before I respond to your proposal, there are some things about my father and me that you ought to know," she said. "And Gabe, if you decide to walk away,

I want you to know that I will not hold you to your offer of marriage."

He looked at her puzzled.

Drawing a deep breath, she said, "For many years my father has been proprietor of some—shall I say—businesses of ill-repute. To be perfectly honest, he was in partnership with another man in tippling shops and wenching houses. Those places were completely acceptable to most of the elite men of Charleston, for they were well known for patronizing them…openly, I might add. My father arranged some business deals with them, to expand his business farther up along the coast. He stole their money and that's why Sweeney and Carlton were sent after him to transport him back to Charleston." She threw a quick glance at him, expecting to find scorn written on his face, however, his countenance remained unreadable.

"There are other things you need to know, things about me in particular. Father never married but was intimately involved with the madam of one of his wenching houses. Her name…."

Abigail stopped in thought. "Her name's not important."

Shifting slightly away from Gabe, she admitted, "However, she was my mother. She died shortly after giving birth to me and father sent me away to Virginia for a few years, until I was nine, actually. Bringing me back to live in Charleston, he hired the best tutors available for me. But at the age when young ladies are presented to proper society, I was not accepted. Because of my background and questionable birth, none of the families felt that I was suitable to marry into their social class."

She cleared her throat. "I ended up teaching the children of the wenches, not the children of the elite.

"Another thing you should know," she uncrossed her arms and rubbed her hands together nervously, "is that I fell in love with one of the sons of the wenches. When Father found out that we were seeing one another—that's when we left."

She paused for a moment. "Well…that's about it."

Looking sideways at her, he asked curiously, "What was the name of the man you were in love with?"

"Were?" she asked.

"Gabe, I still am," she said softly. "I'm still in love with him."

Abigail took a measured breath and said. "If it makes any difference, his name is Phillip."

"Let me ask you something, Abigail."

She looked at him through veiled eyes.

"Do you think you could ever love me? Oh, maybe not the same way you do him. But do you think you could possibly find it in your heart to have some feeling for me?"

"Are you willing to take me that way, Gabe?" she asked, astonished. "Knowing that I love another man?"

Drawing up his knee, Gabe hiked his foot on the log and rested his elbow on his knee. "Tell me, Abigail. If Phillip loved you so much, why didn't he take you away from all that?"

Abigail's eyelids flitted down. She had wondered the same thing, had spent the last year hoping against hope that he would ask. Even when her father found out, she desperately wanted Phillip to leave all and declare his love for her.

"I—I," she stammered, "I suppose he didn't want to leave his family."

Gabe's eyebrows rose a shade.

"How's that, Abigail?" he wanted to know.

She dropped her head. "He's married," she admitted.

"I can't help it, Gabe," she said. "I still love him. Even though I know what I did was wrong. He made me feel special…wanted. I could talk to him. *Really* talk to him. No other man made me feel that way before."

Gabe could feel the tearing of her heart. He knew all too well his own hurting and sensed what she was going through. But, at some point, she had to go on and leave the past behind, no matter how much it grieved her. That much he had learned from his own sorrow. Time didn't stop for anyone. And if all you did was look back and didn't eventually move on, you were lost...lost in the past, while the rest of the world marched ahead, living and loving.

"Well—the way I see it," he eventually drawled, "life is based on the decisions we make. Emotions don't really play into it all that much, not after a while, anyway."

Pity softened his voice, "For all of your father's wrong-doing, he did what was right in taking you away."

Touching her hand, he continued, "Abigail, there are many people that touch our lives in one way or another. I loved my wife. Still do, as a matter-of-fact. But I have room in my heart to love you, too. Can't you see that? Is that so hard to understand?"

She looked at his hand resting on hers.

He asked, "Don't you feel anything for me at all, Abigail?"

"Yes," she answered, "of course I do." "But...do you still want me, now that you know my background?"

"Your past makes no difference to me," he said honestly as he pulled his hand away.

"I've tried to run away from it all," she said.

"I understand that," Gabe answered slowly, "however, we're starting a new life in New Wellington. No one has to know where or what you came from. And if you really think about it, many on this caravan are trying to leave something behind."

She grew thoughtful. "That may be, but I've given a great deal of thought to this since Father was taken away. Who knows when someone from my past will show up? I really think it's best to tell someone and I've been thinking about talking to Reverend Templeton. After all, he's hiring me and I think he has a right to know."

Gabe nodded. "I suppose that's true." His tongue passed over his upper lip. "But, you still haven't answered my question. Will you marry me?"

"Even knowing I still love Phillip?" she asked, searching his eyes.

He looked hard at her. "I had to know," Gabe answered at last.

"And now?" she asked him, her heart beating a little too fast.

"I know all I need to know," he told her.

"Are you sure?" she questioned.

"From the bottom of my heart," said Gabe sincerely.

Abigail laid her hand very gently on his forearm. "Then, if you still want me, yes, Gabe," she said quietly. "I will marry you."

CHAPTER THIRTY-EIGHT

AS SAM WAS OPENING THE BELLS on his cattle, he was pleased as the sound of Rachel's soft laughter reached his ears. That was a sound he hadn't heard for many days. He was glad...glad the angry and grieving look on her face that had been there was finally gone, at least for the moment. Unobserved, Sam leaned back against a tree watching her as she chatted and laughed with the other girls. He chortled quietly when they began dashing water at one another.

Wiping her face, Rachel laughingly informed them, "I don't know about you, girls, but I'm coming back here later for a *real* bath."

Rachel had almost filled the buckets at the river when she became conscious that someone was watching her and she looked quickly to where Sam was lounging against the tree. He wiped the smile from his face, straightened, and turned toward one of his horses.

She paused, becoming perplexed as she thought about him. In spite of two marriages, Rachel didn't know much about the ways of men, but she had the vague feeling that something was different about Sam, different from Peter, and even different, in some way, from Ransom. Just what it was, she couldn't quite put her finger on.

Sam, she knew, was a Christian. It was evident in his behavior toward others. But the way he kept his distance from her, made it clear that he didn't care very much for her. But couldn't he see she was also a Christian? His formality and reserve when he spoke to her was absolutely maddening.

Did he doubt her Christianity? Or was it because she was divorced? Did he even know? And if he knew, was he judging her? Questions tumbled over and over unanswered in her mind. She had desperately wanted to leave Wellington and go to Kentucky for that very reason, to escape the taunts of others. The rest of the trip would be unbearable, if he was secretly judging her wrongly.

Somehow she had to find out—and soon.

Rachel rose up from the ground, and as she did so, she fitted the wooden yoke across her shoulders. Straightening her back, and adjusting her wet skirts, she walked back toward the camp without another glance.

∞○∞○∞○∞○∞○∞○∞○∞○∞○∞○

The night air was thick and stagnant with the sultry heat.

As the long hours passed, Rachel couldn't sleep and wanted to dip into the coolness of the water again. She dressed quickly, reached for her moccasins and slipped them on. Quietly, she climbed out of her tent and as she glanced around, the only stirring she saw was the dancing of amber and red flames in the campfire.

She stood still, listening to the silence of the camp. There was a full moon and a smattering of its light through the trees.

She left the camp and walking beyond the trees into a clearing, a voice behind her called her name, causing her to jump. Turning, eyes wide with terror, her mouth went too dry to utter a sound.

Sam grabbed her arm and in a hushed voice, he exclaimed, "Rachel! Don't be afraid. It's me, Sam."

Expelling her breath, "You nearly scared me to death, Sam," she hissed.

Her entrance into the clearing had surprised him. A vision was what he thought he was seeing. There was a catch in his throat when he realized the lady with the flowing black hair was Rachel.

The moon was full and she frowned at him suspiciously.

"What are *you* doing here?" she asked, lowering her eyes and shaking off his hand. "What do you want?"

"To answer your first question, I'm on sentry duty."

"I didn't think you did guard duty anymore."

Ignoring her remark, "And as far as your second question, I want to know what *you're* doing out here in the dark by yourself?" he demanded.

When she spoke, her voice was tinged with icy coolness.

"I'm not afraid of the dark. Never have been," she told him curtly. Her mind instantly raced back to when she was lost in the forest.

Not much, I'm not.

"That may be, Rachel, but it's not safe out here in the night alone," he informed her.

"Indeed!" she answered. "You can't tell me what to do, Sam Spencer. I'll do what I want and go where I want." Giving him a hard glance, she added, "And it appears I'm *not* alone. After all, *you're* out here on guard."

She scuffed her moccasin on a large rock protruding from the ground.

"Besides, it's so hot and I couldn't sleep," she explained as she closed her eyes, threw back her head, and rubbed her neck.

Sam stared at her thoughtfully.

"Well, then. But it would be better for you to return to camp, Rachel."

She didn't respond. She had no intention of going back. Not just yet. Not until she understood what his problem was.

"This isn't good, Rachel. It's not right for us to be out here alone. Someone might wake and see us and come to the wrong conclusion."

When she didn't answer, "You ought to go, Rachel," he insisted.

Again—no answer, but a defiant crossing of her arms.

The repeating song of a whippoorwill sounded.

Though they had left the Warrior's Path, still, the danger of Indians lurking about was a real possibility.

He drew in a deep breath, and taking an alert glance around, pulled her into the edge of the trees.

He stood, studying her in the dappling shadows of the moonlight through the trees. His mind went quiet and still within, examining the situation.

"Something must be troubling you. Anything you care to tell me about?"

Rachel shifted under his scrutiny. She wasn't expecting such a direct question—actually she didn't know what she expected. Suddenly, she wasn't sure that she had the nerve to ask him why he had been so cold. She didn't know him very well at all. He, in fact, was almost a stranger to her. She merely pursed her lips and shook her head. After all, *he* was the one who had been distant.

"You might as well get out in the open what's on your mind," said Sam quietly as he crossed his arms too.

"Rachel?"

Placing his hands on his hips and giving her a crooked smile, he urged, "Don't let a frown mar that beautiful face of yours."

With a start, she uncrossed her arms and turned her face up to his. His tone surprised her. He had the advantage over her. Her face was turned directly toward the full moon while his back was towards it, so it was hard to see what expression he had in his eyes. She felt he was laughing at her and the thought goaded her.

Irritated, she clenched her fists and began to turn from him.

He enfolded her arm with his hand and tried to reason with her. With playful persuasion in his voice, he exclaimed, "You know…you're too pretty to scowl like that."

"Humph!" she exclaimed in frustration. She was getting confused. He had ignored her and been somewhat cold and distant in the past, now he had done a complete about-face. She didn't know who Sam really was.

He smiled and a little of her nervousness passed. But with him so close, she was put off her mettle, and his nearness made her feel ill-at-ease.

He laughed softly as he navigated in territory familiar from past conquests. Seeing her relax a shade and removing his hand from her arm, he folded his arms once again.

Quietly, he prodded, "Now, suppose you tell me what's wrong."

How could she tell him her thoughts? If he didn't know she was divorced, she didn't want to inform him. She guessed the best course of action was to put *him* on the defensive.

"Let me ask you something, Sam Spencer."

"Yes?" Sam replied and raised his eyebrows, alerted by something in her voice.

She turned to him. "Why don't you like me?"

There. She'd said it.

His thumb tipped back his hat. "Why don't I like you? What do you mean?" Sam questioned. "What makes you think I don't like you?"

Rachel began to fidget and cast her eyes down. "Well—you're often very—very cold toward me," she said. She had to know, even if it hurt. She glanced at him, her head cocked to one side and continued, "Is—is there something you've heard about me?" she asked.

"Rachel," he began, "I must confess…I know practically everything about you…including your divorce, if that's what you're thinking about."

She suddenly felt panicked and could hear her own heartbeat in her ears.

Someone was gossiping about her. But who?

She was looking for a new start away from the criticism of others, but it seemed her past would always follow her.

She had tried, *really* she had, to make a good marriage, but Peter's aspiration was only in the gaming halls, not in the home and, after all, it was her ex-husband Peter who sought the divorce, not she.

Rachel shut her eyes, unable to look at him any longer. Was there anywhere that she could escape from her past? Would this haunt her for the rest of her life? Granted, those who came with them from Wellington did not condemn her. Still, she felt, at that moment, like the Samaritan woman at the well that was scorned by everyone but Christ.

Her nails bit into her hands and turning eyes that had turned black as the night about them, she leaned toward him and asked frantically, "*Who* told you? *Who's* been talking about me?"

"There's no point in knowing who told me." He gave a slight shake of his head and shrugged. "Your past is behind you. Leave it there," he answered.

She drew her eyebrows together as rising temper mixed with injury.

"I *can't*," she stated emphatically.

She was strong…had been through much and survived. But the one battle she fought was rejection.

She was looking for peace and the fact that someone in the company might be talking about her, unsettled her to no end.

Where? What place could she find that would free her from her past? It was following her from Virginia to Green River Country.

He knew everything about her, he said? She began to shake at the thought that this man knew all about her. Not only did she have to remain on the road with him and bear his reproaches, but she'd learned that his property in Stone Valley adjoined hers.

This land she was going to was to be her escape, a new start in life. That Sam Spencer would be living next to her was more than she could bear.

She looked around as the trees cast their black shadows in the moonlight. The trees began to sway, the branches creaking overhead as a strong breeze stirred, and a wild inclination to escape, consumed her. She wanted to yield to the wind and be carried away by it.

As the trees rustled, Sam glanced quickly toward them, instantly alert, his hand reaching toward his rifle. Standing attentive for several moments, the wind died down as quickly as it had come.

The whippoorwill resumed its song. There was no real danger. He laid his rifle down again and turned his attention back to Rachel.

"Rachel?"

The darkness of the night wrapped her mind in a fog. His voice went on in the darkness and she heard words, but they made no sense to her.

He was wrestling with something? It had nothing to do with her? What was he talking about? Nothing to do with her past? He didn't care if she was divorced, he was saying. He in no way judged her. Did not judge! He never acted that way. He was always so indifferent toward her, while showing friendliness to others.

Her mind was leaden with defeat.

I can't think of this now. If I think of this a moment longer, I'll go mad.

Perhaps by some miracle it would all pass. After all, she had staked everything on this trip. Selling her farm, marrying Ransom, making a new start.

He watched her intently for a long time. Rachel gradually became composed, and although her face was pale, her chin had a certain lift to it.

His jaw tightened and he asked, "You're not going to run away?"

She felt exhausted. It was all so mixed up in her mind and she was so tired.

Pushing back her hair with a hand that shook slightly, "No," she answered dully.

He looked as though he didn't believe her, but stated, "Good."

A numbing crept over her heart. Now she knew that someone was talking about her past. She wished she had stayed in camp. Wished she had never found out.

She looked up at Sam, all emotion gone from her eyes. All that remained was a dull ache in her heart.

Picking up his rifle, he told her with all the reserve he could muster, "It's getting late, Rachel. I think it's time that you turn in."

With one final look at him and straightening her back, she turned and walked back toward camp. As long as she lived, Sam Spencer would never get the best of her, she determined.

As she neared the edge of camp, John Winslow stepped out and took her arm.

"Rachel!"

"Pa?" she asked, startled.

"What are you doing out here, Rachel?" he demanded sternly.

"I couldn't sleep, Pa, so I decided to take a walk," she answered.

"I've warned you about being out in the dark alone," he snapped. "You want some Indian buck to carry you off to be his squaw…or worse?"

She dropped her head. "You're right, Pa. I—I wasn't thinking."

John rolled his eyes. "Wasn't thinking? Promise me you won't do this again. I don't have time to watch after you *and* the rest of the party."

"Sorry," she apologized, shaking her head. "I promise, I won't do it again."

He turned her around and said, "Look at me."

She raised her head and he peered into her eyes. "Sam Spencer is on guard duty. Does this have anything to do with him?" he asked pointedly.

As she tried to shift her eyes and pull away from him, John insisted, "Rachel, I want to know, is there something going on? Do you have feelings for Sam?"

At his question, her jaw dropped and her eyes opened wide in shock. "Pa! How could you think such a thing?"

She was aghast. Ransom lay dead in a forlorn grave in Powell Valley. How could her own father, who thought the sun rose and set on her, think such a thought? It was inconceivable.

Reluctantly, she stated crisply, "If you must know the truth, I've been upset because Sam treats me so coldly. I couldn't understand why he doesn't like me and I wanted to know why. It's been bothering me. So much so, that I talked to Ransom about it before he died."

He let go of her arm, and with a queer light in his eyes, questioned, "Did you ask Sam why?"

"Yes."

"What was his answer?"

She threw up her hands in exasperation.

"I don't know. I'd been thinking it was because I'm divorced, but he said that wasn't it. He just kept talking about wrestling with something. Men don't make any sense to me, Pa. I'm as confused now as I was before."

He put his arm around her shoulder and guided her back toward the camp.

"I think I did wrong by keeping you secluded all those years you were growing up. You never had a chance to learn much about the ways of people. Don't think anymore about Sam, Rachel. Just realize that everyone loves you for who you are."

She relaxed against him as they walked. "I love you, Pa." Melancholy came over her. "I don't mean to hurt your feelings— but I miss Mother so much. I wish she was still here with us."

He squeezed her shoulder.

She had just turned seventeen and had so much to discover. What she had learned came the hard way and he was concerned. She needed the wisdom of her mother and he was trying unsuccessfully to take her place.

"Perhaps," he mused, "if I had been there for her all along, things might have turned out differently. But I couldn't stay there with those memories."

But that was all in the past and John Winslow was not one to spend much time on yesterdays.

"I know, girl," he murmured quietly. "I know."

∞∞∞∞∞∞∞∞∞∞∞∞∞∞∞∞∞

After sentry duty, Sam lay in his tent, tossing and turning, unable to shut thoughts of Rachel out of his mind. "So, *that's* what was wrong with her. She thought I was against her because of her divorce. If she only knew...."

Rachel had shaken him to the core of his being. She was the most stubborn and unpredictable female he had ever met. So accustomed was he to game-playing, that he'd become a master of emotional disguise. But he was close to dropping that disguise and that would never do. Better to revert to his aloofness toward her than to get any closer.

"Almost. I *almost* said some things I shouldn't," he thought. He'd always prided himself on his self-control when it came to women and he'd nearly blown it.

"No, that would never do. I'm not interested in marriage or settling down with any one woman...not for the present, anyway. I've got ministry to think about. Not only that, but my estate will take a great deal of my time, in addition to overseeing Rachel's estate. And there's my legal profession in town." he reasoned. "No—there's no time for women in my life. *Especially* not this one."

240

He was angry with John. Why did he let her go out in the dark alone like that where any wild creature could attack her? Well…perhaps he hadn't known.

He sighed, turned onto his back and looked at the ceiling of his tent, his ear attuned for any movement from hers.

"I might as well have stayed on duty for what little sleep I've got."

CHAPTER THIRTY-EIGHT

IT WAS THE MIDDLE OF SEPTEMBER. The party had traveled for several weeks and they had forded rivers and streams, climbed high mountains, and suffered losses along the way.

To some in the party, and especially Jane, it seemed their journey would never end. Though Jane had thrown a fit about being forced to live in a cabin when they reached Stone Valley, after being in a tent for so long, a cabin would seem like one of Wellington's finest homes. There was nowhere to go but forward—always forward.

Seven miles from their destination they came upon a small settlement called Mission Point. Not much of a town—just a few log houses and a tavern that served as a general meeting place.

They had already passed such places, many of them abandoned. Occasionally they came upon a lone cabin with its occupants of mother and children just as lonely as their surroundings, as they were almost literally cut off from civilization. These were dull and dreary women, as though deprived of the company of others the life had been drained from them.

John entered the tavern along with Sam and Will. A tall man with light brown hair and cautious blue eyes approached them.

"Hello, Jubal."

"Been expecting you, John," he said, spitting a wad of tobacco onto a puncheon floor already stained and spotted with sticky gobs of the same. "Have a good journey?"

"Had some trouble on the way. Some people killed."

"Indians?"

"No."

After a few moments of silence, seeing that John wasn't in the mood to elaborate, Jubal asked, "Get you folks a drink?"

"No spirits, Jubal."

"Don't have nothing like that, John," he said. "Just some cider, is all."

John turned to Sam and Will and said, "Sam Spencer, Will Templeton, this here's Jubal Munday. Jubal owns this place."

Intelligent eyes sat quietly in a corner, observing the men as they talked. Though dressed in backwoods clothing, it was apparent the young boy, about five years old, was Indian. Anyone could tell that. But although he had indigo-black hair, the lad had striking blue eyes.

Sam and Will looked curiously at the blue-eyed Indian boy. They had traveled for about a month and hadn't seen hide nor hair of a single Indian on the way. Ironically, now nearing their destination, they find one, and a tame one at that.

Jubal noticed the men staring and remarked offhandedly, "That there's my boy Billy." Noting the startled look on their faces, he said, "His ma was Indian," with a shrug of his shoulders and another spit of tobacco.

"Had any problems with Indians, Jubal?" John inquired.

"No...not for some time now. 'Spect you won't have any reason to worry about 'em, though. Not around here, anyways."

John nodded.

"So, John," Jubal asked, sucking air through his teeth, "how many folk you got in your party?"

John rested his rifle upright on the floor. Crossing his arms across the barrel, he answered, "About two hundred. Planning on establishing a town in Stone Valley. You know...where the Stone boys live. Got the name already picked out for the town. New Wellington, it is."

"Hmm," Jubal said, nodding his head.

"Aim to build a church and school. The whole thing, you know."

"Well...I don't rightly know about church," jerking his head in the boy's direction, "but Billy could use some schoolin'. And the rest of the folk here might be some interested."

John picked up his rifle and laid it in his arms. "Mind if the party camps here tonight, Jubal? Tomorrow being Sunday, we'll most likely head out day after tomorrow."

"Suit yourself, John. I 'spect the rest of Mission Point has already got the news that you're here. Reckon the folks in the hills will be out ter'ectly. Don't see many strangers come through here...especially a preacher. I reckon some will be wantin' to get married."

The party was busily pitching camp as the few one-room, windowless cabins, not very well chinked, offered up their inhabitants through their low doors. Unwashed, bushy-bearded men and tired-looking women with numerous dirty children streaming out behind them, tripping over barking hounds, stared curiously at the goings-on that had come to Mission Point. Never such a crowd of people and cattle had they seen pass through here before.

They had very little to say at first, but eventually warmed to friendly overtures from Jacob and Elizabeth.

Learning that Jacob was a preacher, they immediately pleaded that he hold funeral services for their buried dead. Some had passed away recently and others had been dead for years. The funerals had been delayed for no preacher had passed through the area to preach the services.

Jacob agreed that the next day, Sunday, the services would begin. Word spread quickly for miles around of the "funeral occasion", and many from the surrounding hills as far as ten miles away came for the event, for many families had someone who had passed away. The "occasion" began on Sunday afternoon, and the service lasted several hours with many prayers and hymns. The women shouted and wailed for the dead, some of whom were long departed, as they worked themselves into a fever pitch of emotion.

Several couples asked to be married, and in the evening, Jacob performed the ceremonies.

By the end of the day, the people had lost their shyness with the strangers and told of their family affairs. Many sad stories were heard—how the father drank and whipped the mother or that some folk were killed and strong drink was the cause of it. Mothers, especially, were glad that New Wellington would be settled and their children could now have a chance to become educated. One scrubby little boy, learning that Abigail was the teacher, ran to the creek, and coming back with maiden-hair, proudly presented the fern to her.

"I know our assignment is in New Wellington," remarked a tired Elizabeth after the long day, "but there is work here at Mission Point, also. Don't you agree, Jacob?"

"Absolutely," Jacob concurred. "But our first obligation is to our assignment commissioned by the Organization. He smiled a weary smile and reached over and touched her hand. "After we're settled, we'll see if the Organization might send another schoolteacher. We'll pray that God will somehow work something out. There's much to do and we'll do it, God willing."

Hearing there was a doctor in the party, the locals convinced John to linger one more day. As James assisted Doctor Stone, they flocked to him, as many of them had never been attended by a doctor before.

Early the next morning, the party was restless, anxious to get to Stone Valley. They had traveled a long way and were eager for their journey to end. They needed no encouragement as John gave the word to pack up and get ready to move out.

∞∞∞∞∞∞∞∞∞∞∞∞∞

Arriving at Stone Valley, Rachel dismounted her horse and stood on a rise. As her eyes scanned the valley, she was overwhelmed at the cane that grew there in abundance. So much so, one could easily get lost in it. It was a good land with all manner of trees including oak and chestnut. It was a land of milk and honey just as they had been told—a place where they could forge a new life for future generations. Looking beyond the cane to openings that gave way to forest, she saw open patches of earth sloping down hillsides to rich river bottoms promising abundant harvests.

Fall and Indian summer would soon be here. There was so much to do before the hard freeze of winter set in. Cabins to be raised, fences built, and fall fruit was waiting to be gathered and

246

preserved. Their provisions and possessions would be arriving soon, assuming they had made it to the Falls of the Ohio.

"Oh," thought Rachel, with the first feeling of real pleasure she had experienced since the day she left the farm forever, "I'm going to like it here!"

Rachel's heart began to swell. This was what Ransom had wanted, to start over and build a new life filled with purpose, with her by his side.

They had traveled more than two-hundred and fifty miles. She had been through much—death, denial, desertion, and despair.

"Seasons of change", is what her mother would have said. Change following on the heels of change. And now, surveying the vista before her, she felt hope—hope, firm and unshaken in this new land, a land where she might once again find happiness and contentment.

It was worth everything she had faced, this new beginning. She would miss Ransom acutely, would never forget him. But this was what he wanted, not only for himself, but for her, too. Every inch of land, in the transformation from wilderness to plantation, would be devoted to his memory. A fine house would be built in his honor. She would see to that if it took the last ounce of strength in her body. His hopes and his plans would live on in North Star.

"Oh, Ransom! If you were only here to see this!" she exclaimed softly as her heart quickened its beat.

She heard the sound of footfalls behind her. Turning, expecting her father, it was Sam Spencer that approached.

She turned back, and, without words, he took his place beside her, taking in the scene before them as their shadows fell on the ground, mingling as one.

It was a moment of stillness.

They stood a little apart, merely breathing the stillness, with no thought of any other place than this.

Instinctively, Rachel closed her hand over the locket Ransom had given her.

As though on cue, a gentle breeze began to blow, and on the wings of the wind, Ransom's voice wafted like a symphony playing in perfect harmony in her ears.

"All my love, always."

About the Author

A graduate of Chatfield College and from a family of several ministers, Donna Whitaker has pastored several churches, and served as evangelist, missionary, songwriter, recording artist, musician, and teacher. Speaking at various venues, she has also served as spokeswoman and praise and worship leader with Aglow International, the women's division of The Full Gospel Businessmen's Association.

Donna's own family has a history in the area her novels are set in. Of Scottish descent and the well-known Sinclair family, Donna can trace her ancestor sailing on the ship Loyalty to North America in 1699 and follow her family's progress from Virginia to Adair County, Kentucky in the very early 1800's. Church and courthouse records document Alexander Sinclair, her 4th great grandfather, as an ordained minister of that county.

On her maternal side, Donna is descended from Brigadier General Jesse Richardson, a Revolutionary War soldier who also served under General George Rogers Clark. One of the first settlers of Pulaski County, Kentucky, General Richardson was elected to the Kentucky State Legislature as the first senator of Pulaski and Cumberland Counties in 1800.

Interacting with people from many walks of life has given Donna an understanding of people and helped to make her an effective storyteller.

Donna resides in southern Ohio.

Donna may be contacted at donnajeanwhitaker@gmail.com

www.ingramcontent.com/pod-product-compliance
Lightning Source LLC
Chambersburg PA
CBHW031507210626
46807CB00025B/434